Murder, I Spy

A 1920s historical mystery

A Dora and Rex Mystery
Book 1

Lynn Morrison

Cover design by DLR Cover Designs

Published by

The Marketing Chair Press, Oxford, England

LynnMorrisonWriter.com

Print ISBN: 978-1-7392632-1-8

Contents

To all the women who refuse to let societal expectations dictate their life choices.

Chapter 1
Rex reads the news

The complete upheaval of Lord Reginald's future started the moment he crumpled his newspaper into a ball and tossed it into the terrine of hot porridge sitting in the middle of the dining table.

The dining room of this particular home had seen its fair share of temper tantrums over the years, despite being a study in elegance and simplicity. The walls were painted in a pale sage and the curtains pulled back to let in an abundance of sunlight. High-backed chairs upholstered in cream silk surrounded a long, rectangular table made of oak. Located just off Grosvenor Square in Mayfair, the behaviour of the occupants proved that an excellent address and rich furnishings weren't enough to enforce a stiff upper lip.

That didn't mean, however, that its current owner, the Dowager Duchess of Rockingham, welcomed such behaviour. She was a doyenne of the upper class, known as much for her immaculate style as her encyclopaedic knowledge of England's elite. She much preferred to capture titillating snippets of gossip through her intricate web of informants than witness it from a member of her own family.

When the aforementioned broadsheet landed with a splat, sending a glop of porridge onto her starched white linen tablecloth, she was less than pleased. She arched an eyebrow at the fair-haired man seated across from her while the footman rushed to remove the offending object.

"Was the news not to your liking, dear, or was it the porridge? If you want extra seasoning, you need only to send word to Cook."

Lord Reginald, known to friends and family more simply as Rex, flushed in embarrassment. He'd been so engrossed in the paper, he'd quite forgotten his grandmother was still sitting at the table.

"Apologies, Grandmama. There's nothing wrong with the food." Rex speared a bite of egg with his fork to emphasise his point. "It's this situation with Freddie that's causing me indigestion."

His grandmother's expression softened, the disapproval replaced by genuine sympathy. She rested a hand against the stiff lace of her bodice. "Terrible loss, that is. As if your generation didn't suffer enough death during the Great War. To lose a man such as Frederick Ponsonby to a senseless back alley murder... I still can't imagine what he was doing in such a forsaken place."

"It seems imagination is all we have left. According to the Times, the Yard has run out of leads. They've stamped his file as *death by misadventure, caused by person(s) unknown* and seem content to leave it at that."

The Dowager Duchess shook her silvered head, the diamonds in her hair glittering under the dining room chandelier. "Poor Freddie. He deserved better, although I can't imagine the chief investigator took such a decision rashly. The Ponsonby name is well-regarded, even if the death tax left their

2

coffers dry. I had every faith that Freddie would eventually marry an heiress and resolve the problem."

Rex was less convinced on that front, but otherwise shared his grandmother's disappointment. Freddie had been a good man, one of the best he'd known.

Although Freddie had a reputation for driving fast cars, betting on winning horses, and escorting women with questionable moral codes, Rex saw through to the real truth of his character. Freddie preferred to keep his good deeds out of sight. He'd give you the shirt off his back, and was the first to stand at your side in a challenge. While such efforts guaranteed fast friendships, they did little to rebuild a lost fortune.

Now, he was gone, found dead in the shadows of the Ten Bells, a pub in Spitalfields, with a gunshot through his heart. In an area so packed with people that they lived five or more to a room, somehow no one heard the firing of a gun. It wasn't until the morning after that someone contacted the police, and only then to request they collect the body.

Rex had used his family name to demand access to the investigation files, thin as they were. His daily trips to Scotland Yard yielded little result. It didn't matter what he said. The chief investigator had already decided Freddie's public image was as deep as Freddie got.

He'd poked his finger into Rex's chest and leaned close enough for Rex to smell the onions on his breath. "You lordlings should know better than to venture into the slums. No amount of money will guarantee your protection. Frederick Ponsonby should have kept his wagers to those within his own social class, instead of visiting that pub. Mind you, don't make the same mistake, boy."

Rex's cheeks burned hot as fury stole the words from his mouth. He'd grabbed his coat and swept from the man's office without a backward glance.

Even now, several days later, seated at his grandmother's dining table, the memory galled him.

After the footman poured the dowager a fresh cup of tea, she settled her gaze on her grandson. He was a handsome man, with sharp, angular features and a tall, lean frame. His hair was a pale blond, swept back in a stylish pompadour, and his piercing blue eyes were framed by long, dark lashes. His complexion was wan despite the first blush of a tan, marred by dark circles under his blue eyes. Had he lost weight? She recalled all the meals he'd missed in the last week. She'd thought he was at his club, but now she wasn't so sure.

Man or not, he needed a firm hand to get his life back on track. "I'm sorry to see this terrible tragedy end in such a manner, but at least you can turn your attention to other matters now."

Rex stared, unblinking. "What other matters could be more important than this, Grandmama? My friend is dead. I have no intention of letting the investigation die as well. Not so soon, anyway. There's no way they ran down every lead in such a short time."

His grandmother was unmoved. In a voice as steely as her rigid spine, she replied, "It is done, Rex. Accept his death and mourn him, but your attempts to manoeuvre the team at Scotland Yard are at an end. This level of involvement is unhealthy... Particularly for you." She tilted her head so her stately profile caught the sunlight. "I heard you cry out in your sleep last night. Again. That's the fourth time since you learned of Freddie's death."

"Fifth," Rex whispered, unable to keep the word from slipping from his lips.

"Worse than I feared. I'll ask the doctor to send over a sleeping draught. You will return to your studies. That calmed you before. Take your mind off things." She prattled on as though she were discussing a child and not a man in his mid-twenties.

Rex watched as his grandmother took his future in a firm grip, running ahead with her plans to help him deal once again with the terrors that ruined his sleep. Dreams of battlefields, of narrow escapes. In his mind's eye, the chaos of war shrank until all he saw was a severed limb beside a lifeless body. Worse yet were the nights he dreamt of the living. How many times had he revisited the final moments of those gunned down before his very eyes?

His grandmother was right in one way. He was smart enough to recognise that the only thing that would stave off the horrors in his mind was driving himself to distraction. The Chief Inspector sneered at the inane pastimes of the titled and wealthy, blind to their reasons.

He'd had only to ask the question. Why did young men like Rex and Freddie waste the hours of their days with gambling, drink, women, and dancing?

They were all too aware of just how brief life could be. They knew that there was no explanation or justification for who lived and who died. The unbearable burden of surviving weighed so heavily on Rex's shoulders that his chest grew tight and he heard his heart pounding in his head.

Yet, around the start of spring, something in Freddie had changed. His eyes grew less shadowed, and his laugh less forced.

"What's your secret?" Rex had asked. "Is it a woman? Has the great Freddie Ponsonby fallen to Cupid's bow?"

"Not likely," Freddie had said with a chuckle. "I simply recognised that I'd spent far too long laying amongst the flowers. It was time for me to stand up and be a man."

Rex had scrunched his brow, not understanding what Freddie meant.

Freddie had clapped him on the shoulder, taking pity on his

friend's obvious confusion. "I spent days thinking about those we lost, wondering why me and not them. For a long while, it was more weight than I could bear. But I see now that was wrong. My mourning is done. I decided to live for those who didn't."

"You've revelled in bacchanalia enough for three men," Rex agreed.

Freddie barked a laugh, but his face grew sober. "I must bring balance to my ways. I must be the brother, father, and son. Even if my universe is no larger than the confines of this city, there are still gaps I can fill. I will do what I can, and it will bring me peace."

Their friend Clark had intervened at that point, drawing Freddie away to play the latest parlour game. Rex was left to wonder in what ways Freddie intended to change. He'd longed to ask, but never again found the opportune moment.

Now, he'd never have the chance. Rex knew the truth of what happened in that back alley lay in that very question. Freddie must have been there for a reason. What gap had he seen? Who had he been helping?

Rex's grandmother demanded Rex put those questions aside, but her ask was impossible. Rex had to know. Not just for Freddie.

For himself.

Perhaps the answer would bring meaning to his life as well.

He'd never find out unless he pursued the truth of Freddie's death.

His face hardened into the steely mask he'd perfected on the front lines and he turned his gaze on the woman seated across the table.

The dowager gasped at his transformation.

"I'm no longer a child in leading strings. I will pursue this matter until the bitter end. After all," he added, chuckling darkly, "what are a few nights of lost sleep compared to eternal rest? Do not ask me again to abandon this task."

Her lips flattened into a hard line, but she nodded her agreement.

Rex made quick work of taking his leave from the table and hurrying up the grand staircase to his bedroom suite. His valet was still inside the bedchamber, brushing out the coat Rex had worn the night before.

"Did you need something, sir?" he asked, rising to his feet.

Rex waved at the slender man to keep his seat. "I would never presume to pry into your private life, Brantley, but I'm curious whether you are familiar with anyone in the Ponsonby household."

Brantley paused, brush in hand. "I can't say that I am. You might ask Cook. She has her fingers in a number of pies, if you get my drift."

Rex nodded and turned on his heels to do just that. A wayward thought stopped him in his tracks. He was assuming Freddie's valet might be aware of something because he often confided in Brantley. That kind of narrow thinking was likely why the official investigation came up dry.

"Can I ask you another question? Purely hypothetical," he added.

Brantley set the brush aside and straightened in his chair, giving Lord Rex his full attention.

"If a man were going to choose one person in whom to confide, whom might that be?"

Brantley's shoulders relaxed. "That's easy. He'd tell his wife."

"What if he didn't have a wife?"

"Does he have a woman at all? Anyone he's committed to? If not, I suppose it would be a friend or someone else he trusted. If it's a man of your class you mean, you'd know better than I who else should go on the list."

"Thank you, Brantley. As always, I value your honesty and plain speaking. For a man of my class, as you say, such gems are rare."

Brantley smiled at the compliment. "Is that why you asked me about Ponsonby's household? Are you trying to figure out what happened to him? If so, you might try knocking on the door of his lady friend first. Even if she doesn't know anything, if her photos in the paper are any sign, spending time with her wouldn't exactly be a hardship."

Rex racked his brain but came up short. He paid little attention to the ever-changing rota of women currying favour with their group. "Do you remember her name?"

"I'd be hard-pressed to forget it. Sounds like one of those French film stars. It's Theodora. Theodora Laurent, to be precise. She arrived in London six weeks ago and has been centre stage in many a man's dreams ever since."

Chapter 2
Dora reads the news

Not too far away in an equally splendid, albeit smaller, Belgravia home, Theodora Laurent carried her second cup of coffee and the morning paper to her drawing room. She made it a rule to never mix business with pleasure, and that included not reading the news while nibbling on her toast and egg. Starting the day with a spoilt appetite boded ill for the remaining hours until bedtime.

She moved easily in her simple gown of marron crêpe marocain, a divine creation by the House of Worth that included voluminous sleeves and a sash around the hips. Her favourite chair sat in a puddle of warm morning sunshine, with a maple side table nearby to provide a resting place for her bone china cup. After taking a seat and skimming the first three pages, she dispelled the calm atmosphere with a dark laugh.

"What is it today, Dora? A mishap in the White House? A scuffle in the French parliament? Or did you make it past the international pages before something amused you?"

Dora lifted her emerald-eyed gaze from the paper and batted her lashes at Inga Kay, her dearest friend and companion. "Am I so predictable, darling girl? I'll have to make a point of keeping my amusement to myself moving forward. But to answer your question, it was a short article on the Ponsonby case which caught my eye."

Inga dropped the latest issue of Vogue on her lap. "Freddie's case? Have they identified a suspect?"

"Unfortunately not. However, I'm not so sure that's an accident. I see the invisible hand of Lord Audley in between the lines. The investigation is being shelved as unsolved and the investigators reassigned to other cases. My guess is that is to free the way for Audley to find someone to explore the matter from the safety of the shadows."

"That's good news for us," Inga said. "I can hardly believe the man is dead. To see someone of Freddie's ilk shot like a common thug in a deal gone wrong is beyond the pale. I imagine Lord Audley took the news hard. He'd had such hopes for the man."

"Mayhap that was the problem. Audley offered Freddie the chance to aid England's cause. I doubt he expected his first assignment to be squiring me around town. I never should have told Freddie how I got my start. He must have got it into his head to take a risk of his own. I only wish I knew why he was at that pub. But when he came by, I was sick, and he kept whatever he was planning to himself. Instead of talking to Lord Audley, he took matters entirely into his own hands."

"And for that, he wound up dead. I'll have to remember to add him to my nightly prayers."

Dora couldn't stop a laugh from bubbling from her lips. "Your nightly prayers? I'd say fortnightly, at best."

Inga's brown eyes narrowed as her expression hardened into a glare. "Anyone living with you like I have for the past five years would have need for a word with the heavens now and then."

"You've loved every minute, and don't you deny it," Dora

replied without missing a beat.

Inga winked at her and resumed perusing the magazine. She had little interest in fashion herself, but nestled in between the articles on hemlines and advertisements for face cream, one never knew what they might find in the background of those society photographs.

The two women sat in comfortable silence, each skimming their chosen periodicals for updates and information. An outsider peeking through the window would be hard-pressed to understand the friendship between seemingly polar opposites. Theodora Laurent was every inch the femme fatale, from her strawberry blonde pin curls to her diamond-encrusted ebony earrings. Even when relaxing in her own home, she never let down her guard or her hair.

Inga Kay was almost a decade older, with the first fine lines bracketing her warm brown eyes. She'd brushed her auburn hair smooth and pulled it into a simple chignon. Her sedate dress and wool cardigan allowed her to fade into the background when standing near her glamorous friend. It was as much by design as by preference. Five years earlier, fate saw them assigned the same boarding room near the front lines, but it was a shared like-mindedness and dogged determination that facilitated their friendship.

That, and contempt for the status quo.

A traitorous crime had catapulted the women from battlefield nurses to undercover spies. The Great War was over, but the political machinations that led to its start were far from done. The Crown might not publicly acknowledge their service, but it didn't make their work any less important.

After four years of cavorting around the world's capital cities, they'd finally demanded a well-earned break and had moved closer to home. It was ironic that the world believed this to be Miss Laurent's first visit to England's shores.

According to the rumour mill, Theodora was French or Swiss. Those more envious of her natural charms argued she was nothing more than an American with an exceptionally good tutor. They all agreed she'd come into wealth by marrying and burying a French aristocrat. They were all a little right, but mostly all so very wrong.

No one, not even her family, could have guessed the whole truth of her existence. Dora had always preferred it that way. But somewhere between the hours spent in smoky nightclubs and candlelit dining rooms, Dora had developed a strange itch. After much soul-searching, she forced herself to look in the mirror and admit the truth. She longed for home. While she could never go back to her old life, there wasn't any real reason Theodora Laurent couldn't spend a season in London. Or maybe even two...

After much conniving and careful manipulation, Lord Audley had agreed to a sabbatical of sorts, if such a thing existed in the spy world. One rental agreement and wagon-load of antiques later, there she sat in a Belgravia home worthy of both her real and assumed identities.

"Who do you think Audley will send over next to play the role of my beau?" Dora wondered aloud, once again getting Inga's attention. A rap on the door prevented either from guessing.

The butler, clad in pressed black trousers, white shirt, black coat, and a shocking purple paisley waistcoat, carried a silver tray holding a dingy envelope. "A message for you, madam. Courtesy of the vegetable and fruit seller, so please excuse its appearance."

He was a tall, imposing figure, with broad shoulders and a muscular build. His chiselled jawline was accentuated by a neatly trimmed beard. Housemaids about town swooned at the sight of him, but he only had eyes for the no-nonsense brunette sitting across from Dora.

A well-trained butler would have exited the room at this point, leaving his mistress to read her correspondence in private. While Harris could perform the role to the highest standard, his training had been rather more unorthodox. Besides answering the door and overseeing the household, he also drove a mean getaway car and could be called upon to act as a sharpshooter in times of dire necessity.

Therefore, he was as interested in the contents of the secret communication as the women.

Dora took her silver letter opener from the side table drawer and used it to break the plain wax seal. The paper inside was equally nondescript and contained a few short lines of text.

For the benefit of the others, Dora read it aloud. "I cleared the road and beg you to see where it ends. Proceed with caution. Consider this a favour." She flipped to the other side, but it was blank.

"Would it kill the man to speak plainly for once?" Inga groaned.

"It might, if someone intercepted the letter before delivery. Besides, the message is as clear as the nose on your face." Dora folded the page and passed it back to Harris for destruction. "Audley wants me to find out what happened to Freddie."

"Oh, I understood it," Inga grumbled. "And he framed it as a favour so you'd have no choice but to jump at his call. I find it hard to believe, however, that he doesn't have someone better suited to the task. We've been here for hardly more than a month and are still getting our house in order. You've no network of informants, nor any entrée into society. Not anymore, anyway."

"You know as well as I that Lord Audley's focus has always been on foreign affairs. As for the rest, that's not slowed our missus before," Harris countered, earning himself a scowl from his love interest.

"Indeed," Dora agreed. "And I appreciate the vote of confidence from at least one person in the room." She graced Harris with a warm smile, rubbing her hands together in delight. "Theodora needs no man to open doors for her. She's bloody well capable of turning the knobs on her own."

"And now she's speaking of herself in the third person!" Inga cast her gaze skyward, looking to the heavens for aid.

Dora rummaged through her side table drawer again, this time retrieving a pen and paper. She handed them to Inga.

"What's this for?"

"Your fortnightly prayer list. You've got both Freddie's soul and mine to add. Any more names and you'll need to write them down."

Harris snickered, earning his own glower from Inga. "Might as well put my name on there, too. Maybe the divine can protect me from you."

"Unless you two have a desire to taste-test my latest batch of poisons, I suggest you move onto safer ground. Like determining our next steps."

Dora and Harris exchanged secret smiles while Inga was busy putting the pen and paper aside. Not that her threat was an empty one. Her nursing experience had proven oddly useful for more sinister activities. She'd been known to dose the food or drink of the oblivious guests whenever it suited their needs. Sometimes she stepped in to make the wary relax or fall asleep. Other times she prepared a mixture capable of felling a foe.

She'd made both Dora and Harris test many of her concoctions so they could learn which specific tastes, colours, and smells to avoid. "If you're going to learn the hard way, it might as well be at home," she'd argued as she handed them a drink or plate of food.

She hadn't killed either of them yet. While the side effects were at times unfortunate, Dora and Harris were confident at this point they knew enough to avoid the worst.

Dora motioned for Harris to sit on the fainting sofa. "Sit down, old man. My neck's getting sore looking up at you."

"Forty is not old," Harris groused. "I may look like a plodder in these duds, but put me in the ring with any man and he'll be the one to end up embracing the canvas."

He flexed his arms and did as he was bade, breaking the cardinal rule of never sitting in front of the lady of the house. In the privacy of this home, the trio stood on equal ground. They set all ceremony aside unless an outsider was in their mix.

They were soon well on their way to compiling a list of ideas about how to start on Dora's new assignment.

"Those lads I interviewed for the role of footmen grew up in the slums," Harris offered, tapping the cleft in his square chin. "I'll see how soon they can start and then brief them on their off-the-books tasks."

Inga nodded her approval, having also met the strapping young men. "Handsome twins, smart as a whip, and perfect so long as they don't open their mouths in the dining room."

A brusque knock on the front door echoed in the foyer, interrupting any further plotting. Both Harris and Inga looked at Dora, but she could only shake her head. They weren't expecting any visitors. It wasn't even proper visiting hours.

Harris leapt to his feet and smoothed both his coat and his countenance, wiping away all signs of relaxation. He strutted out of the room to see who it was.

Inga also rose from her chair and went to the window, positioning herself so she could peer out without being seen. They could hear Harris's part of the conversation with their unexpected guest.

"Wait here, your lordship, and I'll see if she's entertaining visitors today."

Dora patted her curls and pinched her cheeks before turning to see why Inga was lingering beside the velvet drapes.

Inga's face had drained of colour, her mouth left hanging half open in disbelief. Harris was barely through the door to the drawing room before Inga blurted, "She'll see him," and waved him back out again.

"What?" Dora hissed, confusion and concern flitting across her delicate features in equal measure.

Inga grabbed the empty coffee cup from the side table and beat a hasty retreat, using the hidden servant's doorway on the far side of the room.

Heavy footsteps drew Dora's attention back to the main entrance, leaving her feeling as though she were watching a tennis match. She did not know which way to look next.

Harris stepped through the doorway, blocking her view. She pasted a blasé smile on her lips and shifted imperceptibly to make the most of the natural light still pouring through the window.

Behind Harris was a debonair man in his mid-twenties. His blond hair was combed away from his forehead, allowing his brilliant azure eyes to be the first thing people noticed.

Dora barely caught herself before her mouth fell open. She swallowed to cover her shock at seeing a ghost from her past striding into her London home.

"Madam, may I present Lord Reginald..."

"Bankes-Fernsby," Dora interrupted, stealing the words from Harris's mouth. Without missing a beat, she crossed the room to slide her hand through his arm and pull him into her web. "My, that's a mouthful. Your friends call you Lord Rex, and so shall I. It's what Freddie would have wanted. I'm sure of it."

Chapter 3
They dodge a bullet

Rex was so overwhelmed by the gorgeous creature that he allowed her to lead him across the room to a sofa that was little wider than an armchair. Nonetheless, Dora sat beside him and wiggled into position, placing them so close together that their knees were touching.

She looked him in the face, batting her thick lashes at him as she waited for him to explain why he was there. But the fact of the matter was that Rex had no idea any longer why he was there. All rational thought had fled from his mind at the first whiff of her perfume and a glimpse of her beautiful face.

Although, now that he was sitting so close to her, he could see her youthful beauty wasn't entirely owed to her looks. Put together, she was certainly stunning. He could understand why Brantley and the others had been so captivated by her photographs in the newspaper.

In person, her desirability owed as much to the thick fringe of lashes around her jade eyes and cupid's bow mouth as to the perfume that filled the surrounding air with hints of hothouse roses. But mostly, it was the intensity of her gaze which drew you in and wiped all rational thought from the mind. When she stared deeply into his eyes, he felt as though they were the only two people in the world.

Flummoxed, Rex let the silence linger a moment too long, leaving Dora to take control of the conversation.

"I assume you've come to check on me after what happened to poor dear Freddie. Such a terrible, terrible tragedy. I can't even imagine what he was doing there. If I'd gone out with him that night as planned, perhaps it would be him sitting here with me now instead of you." Dora's lower lip trembled as she clung to his arm. "Not that I'm not perfectly grateful to have you here with me, Lord Rex. But... well... you know what I mean."

Rex took one look at the unshed tears glittering in her eyes and felt his heart clench. The melodic lilt in her accent and the tremble in her voice proved to be his undoing. "Err, yes," he said, unsure to which of her statements he was responding. He cleared his throat and sat up straighter. "Yes, it is a great tragedy. What happened to Freddie is why I'm here now."

Rex planned to say more, but Dora prattled on, cutting him off mid-word.

"My relationship with Freddie only lasted for a few weeks, but you know when you meet the right person, a few days can feel like a lifetime. I spent the week following his death crying in my room. Today is the first day I've really got up again and only because my companion, Miss Kay, demanded that I do so. Although I hate to admit it, I'm sure that she's right. I'm far too young to spend my whole life mourning. As she says, I'm sure eventually I'll meet someone else who's half as good a man as Freddie. I don't aspire to more than that, because it's practically impossible." Dora dashed a tear from her cheek. "But here I am babbling on when, of course, you knew Freddie longer and I'm sure you're much more distraught than I am. I'm so glad you've paid me a visit so we can sit beside one another and share recollections of Freddie. I'm sure you have heaps of stories from your adventures growing up. Wasn't Freddie the most droll individual you'd ever met in your life, Lord Rex?"

Rex nodded his head to buy time for his brain to catch up. He'd come intending to ask her questions and now found himself entirely on the back foot. He went from barely getting a word in edge-wise, to wanting to tell her everything that crossed his mind. He slid his gaze from her face to the frieze carved above the doorway in an effort to extract himself from her influence.

"Freddie certainly livened up the room, and he'll be missed by all who held him in high esteem," Rex agreed. "I must say, I was unaware the two of you were so close. He'd been keeping you to himself, for the most part."

"I wanted to get settled before I threw myself headfirst into the social scene," Dora explained. "Neither Freddie nor I were the type of individual to pledge our undying devotion. However, I do wish he'd died with the knowledge that I did genuinely care for him, even if our romance was still in the early days. Instead, when he stopped by that evening, I could barely rouse myself from my bed. I came downstairs long enough to tell him I was still unwell and to go on without me."

"The night of his death?" Rex repeated. "You two had plans?"

"Yes," Dora replied, her expression free of guile. "We'd planned a lovely night, but I had a dreadful case of the sniffles that refused to go away. He left me on my own, snuggled under a wrap, holding a steaming cup of tea and lemon. That was the last I saw of him. I could hardly believe my ears when the news arrived two days later."

Rex could barely believe his good fortune. He'd had a distant hope that Freddie's paramour might recall something of value. But to be one of the last people to see him alive?

A dozen questions flitted through his head. What were

Freddie's last words? Did he say where he was going? Who was he planning to meet? Did she have any idea why Freddie would have visited the slums instead of going to one of his usual haunts?

Before he could ask any of them, Dora stood and crossed the room to pull the bell for the butler. The man appeared in the doorway moments later, pushing a trolley cart laden with a pot of tea, two cups, and an array of crumbly biscuits.

"Oh, you brilliant, brilliant man!" Dora exclaimed in delight. "Harris, you always anticipate my every request, sometimes before the thought even crosses my mind."

Harris gave a single nod of agreement. Without a word, he laid the tea and biscuits out on the low table in front of the sofa and exited the room, taking the trolley with him.

Egads, was the man wearing a purple waistcoat? How had Rex missed that when he'd answered the door?

"I'll play mother," Dora offered. "How do you take your tea?"

"Just a spot of milk and no sugar," Rex answered.

Dora raised her eyebrows. "No sugar? I do hope you'll permit yourself to indulge in the biscuits. They were Freddie's favourites. I can't imagine how he remained so fit given his sweet tooth. He always asked for at least four lumps in his cup, and not one less."

Rex laughed as a series of recollections came to mind. He and his friends had always given Freddie a hard time for taking so much sugar in his tea. Freddie had explained that he was simply making up for what amounted to little more than dirty water they'd suffered through while stationed on the front lines. He figured life owed him an extra lump or two to bring balance back to his world.

Dora's knowledge of how Freddie took his tea was a good

sign. They'd obviously spent time together. Otherwise, how would she know?

While Dora busied herself preparing cups of tea and little plates of biscuits for each of them, Rex looked around at the drawing room. What could he glean about the woman from her decor?

Although he'd had the good sense to chat with his grandmother before he'd dashed out of the house, she'd known remarkably little about Theodora Laurent. According to her, Theodora had arrived straight from Paris, where she was the darling of the jazz scene. She had a reputation for being independent and a touch wild, although, thus far, she'd kept that side of her personality under wraps. In her six weeks in London, she'd been spotted a few times going to the opera or dancing the night away in Freddie's arms.

When she'd gone to ground for a week, society made note of her absence. His grandmother thought that perhaps the pair had been on the verge of a split, but now Rex knew the truth. Theodora had simply been ill.

Much like his grandmother's limited knowledge, the drawing room provided only a surface-level insight into its owner's reputation, rather than the woman herself. Where his grandmother preferred Georgian and Victorian furniture, heavy with its ornate details, Theodora's tastes ran more austere and exotic. Paintings of Japanese cherry trees graced the walls and the vase on the mantle was almost certainly from the Ming Dynasty.

Without asking permission, he got up and crossed over to inspect the curio cabinet. The items shared a common theme of couples in love, ranging from porcelain figurines to wooden carvings. He was powerless to stop the blush stealing across his cheeks when he noticed one of the miniature couples was sharing a particularly intimate embrace.

That solidified his decision not to return to the seat on the narrow sofa. Cup of tea be damned. Her floral perfume and the brushing of their knees made his reason flee. He was certain that was by design.

Distance was his ally. He wasn't here to court her, after all. He was here to find out what she might recollect about Freddie so that he could begin his investigation.

He adopted a relaxed pose, resting his elbow on the mantle, and resumed their conversation. "I hope the police didn't badger you too much with their questions."

"The police?" Dora gazed at him over the top of her teacup. "I haven't spoken with anyone other than you about Freddie. As I said, I wasn't with him that night."

"But you were surely among the last to see him," he countered. "They should have contacted you to see if he'd given any indication of his plans... Had he?"

Dora artfully shrugged her shoulders and shook her head. "He said the Great Smoke offered plenty of venues for entertainment. Although my home was his first choice, he was sure he could find an alternative. He mumbled something about a tip on a horse.... I wasn't paying much attention, to be honest. I had a fierce headache."

Rex couldn't hide his dismay. He'd considered Theodora important enough to be his first stop, and the police hadn't bothered to contact her at all. Who knew what she might remember from their conversation, given the proper incentive?

"Did I say something wrong?" Dora asked, interrupting his thoughts. "You're frowning."

"It's not you," he answered in a rush. "I'm frustrated with our police force. They've shelved the case, despite not doing their due diligence. They should have interviewed you."

"Me?" Dora fluttered her lashes again and laid her hand against her chest. "I hardly know a thing! As much as I hate to see Freddie's killer go free, I'm sure the police have their reasons."

"I'm curious about what those reasons are. I'm sorry, Miss Laurent, but I'm going to have to ask you to go to the station with me. We'll go together and tell them you had a conversation with Freddie shortly before his death, and they will have to listen."

Dora's gaze darted back and forth, and her mouth thinned into a tight line. "I'm not sure. Might it be dangerous?"

"Not with me beside you. I'll have you in and out again in no time flat."

Dora placed her cup and saucer on the table and rose from the sofa. Her skirt swayed in time with her slender hips while she approached him. She didn't stop until she was close enough for the edge of her skirt to touch his trousers.

Rex had to tilt his head down to look her in the eye, although not very far. Seated, she gave the impression of being a songbird in need of protection from the big world. Standing, her gamine limbs hinted at strength and poise.

Dora trailed a finger along the lapel of his jacket. "There's no need to leave the comfort of my home. Call the police, if you must, but demand they come here. In the meantime, we can get better acquainted with one another, and speak of Freddie."

Rex gulped, fighting to keep his senses. "You'll speak with them?"

"If I must," she said, shrugging with nonchalance.

"Then let us go. They've wasted enough time as it is. It will be better for everyone if we take the matter to the station. They might ignore a call, but they won't turn us away. Sooner done, the sooner Freddie's murderer is caught."

Dora's moue communicated her distaste with the plan, but she didn't argue. "If you insist. Start the car. I'll collect my hat and wrap and meet you outside."

Rex did as she asked. It took but a minute to get the engine purring.

Dora emerged with a felt cloche covering her strawberry-blonde bob and a Chinese silk scarf wrapped around her shoulders. She paused beside his door to get a good look at the car. It was a Rolls-Royce Silver Ghost.

"Is this the 1921 model?"

"1922," Rex answered, running his hands around the steering wheel in pride. Ever since his father had bought him his first car, he'd taken great satisfaction in having the latest and greatest. "I have a Fiat 510 at home. If you like cars, I'll take you out for a spin in it."

A sharp report ripped through the air. On instinct, both Rex and Dora ducked their heads. The bullet whistled past, taking out the front entry lamp at the house next door.

Dora wrenched open the car door and shoved Rex to the side with a surprising show of strength. With barely a backwards glance, she shifted the car into gear and pulled out into the street, blaring the horn to warn oncoming traffic.

Rex's heart raced as she took the corner on two wheels. "Someone shot at you!"

"At us," Dora corrected. "And unless I'm mistaken, they're following us to see the job done."

Chapter 4
Dora takes a spin

"Have you ever driven a car before?" Rex asked, his hands gripping onto the wooden dash for dear life.

"A time or two," Dora replied, before adding a wink. A time or two thousand was more accurate. Dora chuckled under her breath while shifting the six-cylinder engine into fourth gear and speeding through the tail end of her turn.

Under the guise of another love affair, that time with a member of the Bugatti racing team, Dora had mastered the art of driving under even the most difficult of circumstances. After the hairpin turns and sheer cliffs of the Dolomites, the streets of London proved little challenge.

That left Dora's razor-sharp mind free to focus on other matters. Had the shooter been aiming for her or for Rex?

Their heads had been close enough together that she wasn't sure which one of them the shooter intended to hit. Thinking back, she wondered if the shooter hadn't been aiming for them at all, but had merely fired a warning shot across the bow.

As she'd leapt into the car, she'd barely had time to glimpse the man holding the gun. He'd stood up the road beside a black Tin Lizzie, and if she wasn't mistaken, held a standard British-issue *Smelly* rifle, pointing in their direction. The lack of subsequent fire reassured her greatly. The shooter must have left off the magazine, intending to accomplish his task with a single shot.

Now that they were on the road, the gun was far too inaccurate to risk firing from a moving vehicle in a busy city like London. Dora deemed it safe enough to chance a look back. The Tin Lizzie was two cars back, still in hot pursuit.

Dora took her third left turn in a row. To anyone else, her route would have seemed random, but Dora knew exactly what she was doing. The first landmark she intended to visit was her own home, where she hoped Inga or Harris might catch sight of their pursuer. To be on the safe side, she sounded the klaxon as she sped past and waved.

Rex muttered a string of curse words. "Sorry old girl," he apologised for his ungentlemanly behaviour, before adding a command for her to pull over.

His request fell on deaf ears. Dora had no intention of relinquishing the wheel to him. She knew he'd been a courier for at least part of the war, but ferrying men and messages across the French countryside was a far cry from racing between the double-decker buses, lorries, and the smattering of horse-drawn carriages filling London's busy streets.

"I can't!" she answered, her voice growing higher in pitch as if she were frightened. "What if they shoot at us again?"

When another shot ricocheted off the rear of the car, it was almost as if Dora was prescient.

"My car!" Rex cried, and then punched his fist into his hand in frustration.

"Better the car than our heads," Dora mumbled. She and Rex needed some place safe where they could go to ground. Both their homes were out of the question. They'd catch a bullet before they made it out of the car.

Dora steered the Rolls-Royce onto the wider road at Lower Grosvenor Place. Buckingham Palace was a stone's throw away, but she doubted His Majesty's forces would react favourably to someone aiming for the front gates.

She narrowly missed running down a horse and cart near the Victoria Theatre. There were far too many people bustling to and fro from Victoria Station and the surrounding shops. Dora wasn't entirely sure Lord Audley could convince the law turned a blind eye if she injured a pedestrian.

The thought of the gates gave her an inkling. There was another part of London where one might find an overabundance of guarded gates and burly men.

"Rex, darling, does your family invest in any of the warehouses down by the docks?"

"You want to take a ship?" His bewildered stare made it clear he had no clue why she was asking.

"The original proverb says that in adverse circumstances one welcomes any source of respite, but I've always preferred the more colloquial version..." Dora waited for Rex to catch up before adding, "Any port in a storm? Does your family have access to any berths or not?"

Dora pushed on the brake and skidded around a mother pushing a perambulator. The Vauxhall Bridge was up ahead. Traffic was light enough that she could make the most of the speed the Rolls-Royce offered. However, there was nothing to slow their pursuers. They needed a hideout, ideally sooner rather than later.

Rex's Adam's apple bobbed as he came to grips with their situation and what Dora was asking him. He rested his fingers on his temple and tensed his hand as though he was physically prying the answer from his mind. "Yes!" he shouted in elation. "Near Battersea. Turn right when we get over the bridge."

Dora patted herself on the back for the time she'd invested

in her first week learning the lay of the land. She'd visited London several times as a child, but her parents had limited her world to places they thought appropriate for a girl of her age and station. Nothing near Vauxhall had made that list.

"Where do we turn next?" Dora asked. When Rex failed to reply, she glanced over at her erstwhile companion to see what was the problem. She found him staring out the front windshield, his gaze skipping wildly from one side of the road to the other. The man was most definitely in over his head.

A quick word to buck up his spirits was in order. However, that approach carried a risk. In time, Rex would think back to this moment. Did she want him remembering her as surprisingly competent in the face of incredible danger?

That was out of the question. Therefore, she had to find another way to calm him down. Based on her experience, which was shockingly broad given her age, there were only two types of people who walked blithely into danger. The first group was those who had specialist training and knew how to minimise their personal risk.

In other words, people like her.

Since revealing that was out of the question, she had to turn to the more unpalatable option for solving her current predicament.

She was going to have to act like a senseless fool and hope chivalry would spark some bravery on his part.

She forced the disgusted curl in her lip to twist into a giddy grin. "Darling, isn't this just like one of your car rallies? Freddie regaled me with stories all about them, and I was desperate to attend the next one. Now here I am in the centre of London doing just that."

Rex shook himself free from reverie and turned to face her. He caught one glimpse of her toothsome smile and promptly lost the plot.

"Are you mad, old girl? Do you think this is some kind of lark? People are shooting at us! They could kill us."

"I know! It's absolutely divine! It's the perfect je ne sais quoi to bring a sense of verisimilitude to the entire experience. I can't wait to get home and tell Inga all about it. You'll have to come along and back me up. I can already imagine her accusing me of fabricating the finer details."

Rex's gaze burned the side of her head, but Dora didn't mind. She'd accomplished her goal. When she turned and met his glare, her smile was genuine.

Rex loosened his grip on the dash long enough to throw his hands up in the air in frustration. He wiped a hand down his face and finally clocked in to their surroundings. "It's the next street on our right."

"I do love a good right turn," Dora replied, her tone belying the utter inanity of her words. "Hang on. I dare not slow down."

Rex chanced a look out the window as they made the turn. He thought he spotted their pursuer, but he couldn't be sure. There were far too many black cars in London.

"Hurry," he urged Dora. "Straight ahead, pull in through the gates."

Dora pressed on the horn, emitting a warning toot to passersby. She barely slowed long enough to wave at the man watching the car sail through the gate.

Every worker in sight stopped what they were doing and turned to watch the spectacle.

And what a spectacle it was!

The silver Rolls-Royce was worth more than any of those men earned in a year. The infamous Theodora Laurent was immediately identifiable, thanks as much to the jaunty grin on her face as the ebony and diamond earrings flashing from under her strawberry blonde curls.

Dora barely took her foot off the accelerator as she

manoeuvred around the docks. She finally brought the car to a stop after driving up a loading dock into the safe confines of a towering warehouse.

Rex's hand trembled and his heart still raced inside his chest, going faster than the thoroughbred steeds at Ascot.

While he sought control, Dora's expert gaze skimmed the warehouse contents. When she saw the label stamped on the side of a box, an idea came to mind.

"A gin warehouse! Aren't you clever!" she cried. "I'm simply gasping for a drink and I daresay there's enough here to wet an army." She flagged down a worker. "Be a good man and load a crate into the back for us. Lord Rex here will sign for it, won't you, darling?"

The man, tall and muscular, hoisted a crate and circled the car. "You've got a spot of damage here, your lordship."

Dora opened her door and slithered from behind the wheel, swinging her hips while she circled around to the rear. The shudder of the car door closing rocked Rex back to the present. He opened his door and followed suit.

Dora fluttered her lashes at him. "Oops! You'll probably want to have this repaired. Shall we leave your car here, Rexy-dear, and borrow one from the lot?"

Rex stared, dumbfounded, at the perfect circle marring the shiny silver panel.

"Lord Rex?" Dora called his name again to get his attention. "Being seen in a damaged car could be detrimental to our reputations... if you know what I mean."

Rex blinked a few times as the meaning set in. Of course, Theodora was right. If they hoped to make it to safety, they needed to go incognito.

Dora clapped her hands in delight when Rex straightened his shoulders and blazed ahead, backing up her ridiculous behaviour.

"Right-o, that's a brill idea. Ready a car and include the crate. After the morning we've had, a glass of gin is the least of what we'll need."

Dora swayed close and looped her arm through Rex's. "I know exactly where we can get some tonic to go with it. For our health," Dora added. "I'll even let you drive this time."

If Dora's chest brushed against Rex's arm, she could hardly be blamed for using every tool at her disposal. "In moments like this, I can't help but remember an old Chinese saying."

Rex raised his eyebrows at the woman hanging from his arm.

"The gem cannot be polished without friction, nor man perfected without trials. Buck up, Lord Rex. With any luck, we'll turn our coal of a morning into a diamond before night falls."

Chapter 5
Rex loses an argument

Their return trip across the river was decidedly less noteworthy. Within twenty minutes, Rex drew the drab black Model T he'd borrowed to a stop on Gerrard Street in Soho.

"Are you sure this is where you want to go?" Rex asked, eyeing the dark windows at the front of the building. The number forty-three above the door proclaimed both the address and the name of the establishment. "The dancing won't start for hours."

"That's what makes this the perfect place for us to hide out while we discuss our next steps. No one will think to look for us here, not for hours yet, if at all."

Rex was unconvinced. He approached the main entrance and was dismayed to find it locked. He turned to face Dora and saw her standing there with her handbag open and a ring of keys in hand.

"Mrs Meyrick and I are dear friends," she explained while she searched for the correct one.

Rex was loath to admit it, but he didn't believe she was telling the truth until the key twisted in the lock.

The owner of the 43 Club greeted them as soon as they came through the door. Middle-aged, but with the energy of a young woman, she dropped her paperwork to rush over and give Dora a kiss on either cheek. "Theodora, you're a sight for sore eyes. You graced our premises twice in the same week and then disappeared. I feared you'd found someplace else to cool your heels."

"As if anything could compare to the 43!" Dora trilled, waving off the mere suggestion. "I was under the weather, and that was before I heard the news about Freddie. Speaking of Freddie, Kate, do you know Lord Rex?"

"Of course, although not as well as you do, if your appearance at this ungodly hour is any clue." Mrs Kate Meyrick, a nightclub owner as famous as her clientele, was happy to welcome them both. Her indefatigable spirit and stiff upper lip had earned her a reputation as a keeper of secrets. Not even a stint in the gaol had been enough to quell her determination to support the jazz scene.

She escorted them deeper into the club and motioned to the empty tables. "Have a seat and I'll see if Maurice can put together a tray of sandwiches for you. I'd offer you a drink, but thanks to the lawmakers, it will be hours before I can bring it over."

"A bottle of tonic and two glasses will be good enough," Dora replied. "If you wouldn't mind sending someone out to fetch the crate from the car, we'll take care of the rest ourselves. There's plenty enough to leave something behind as payment for your troubles."

Kate raised her eyebrows and left to comply with the unorthodox request.

Rex made himself comfortable in the wooden chair. While Dora did the same, he took advantage of the opportunity to see the club in the daylight hours. The wooden panelling, simple furniture and checked tablecloths belied the bar's status. The owner knew the walls had no need for further adornment.

Once night fell, all eyes would be on either the mirror above the bar or on the brass instruments gracing the stage. The club was normally heaving with men and women dressed to the nines. Now, the place felt forlorn in its emptiness.

He'd visited before, but this wasn't one of his regular haunts. The set at the 43 ran faster than he preferred. Visitors were just as likely to rub elbows with the members of the House of Lords as the heads of the crime syndicates.

In some ways, knowing Theodora felt at home in its environs made perfect sense. Her familiarity, however, was at odds with her brief stay. "I thought you'd only been in London for a month."

"I have," Dora answered, after pausing to say thanks to the young man who delivered a tray of sandwiches. "I make it a point of forming fast friendships with the right sort of people. Useful people," she added, wiggling her eyebrows.

Rex did not know what to make of that comment. He could think of plenty of reasons a seductress like Miss Laurent would cosy up to a nightclub proprietress. However, when he looked into Theodora's emerald eyes, that knowledge flew right out the window.

Already, their mad adventure was fading in his memory. Had they really turned the streets of London into a race track and outrun a man with a gun? The entire event flickered soundlessly in his mind like scenes from a moving picture.

Theodora sat across from him, nibbling at the edge of a cress sandwich. How was it possible that she looked both angelic and somehow incredibly human at the same time?

Then she raised her gaze and looked him full in the face. Her lips quirked up as though she was recalling some private joke. Perhaps she was. Rex certainly couldn't hazard a guess at what passed through her mind. One moment she was a steady hand on the wheel and the next a devil-take-care delight.

She was an enigma.

Rex's admiration for Freddie soared to uncharted heights. His childhood friend had not only caught the attention of the minx, but impressed her enough that she mourned his passing.

Where did the artifice of Theodora Laurent stop and the real woman begin?

Rex tamped down any thoughts of finding out. He was not Freddie. When it came to Theodora, to all of this, really, he was in over his head. It wasn't right for him to drag her into trouble. He owed it to Freddie to keep her safe.

"This has to stop."

Dora paused with her hand on the top of the gin bottle. "Don't tell me you can't use a drink after the adventure we had!"

"What? No, that wasn't what I meant." Rex nudged his glass closer. "I owe you an apology, Miss Laurent. I knocked on your door and roused you from the safe confines of your home. You were shot at, chased, and nearly lost your life. I'm entirely to blame, and I'll understand completely if you never want to see me again."

"Nonsense! What is life if not for living? Today's antics hardly rate a mention in my diary. Being chased by a pack of lions while on safari... now that got my heart racing! Charles, Cottar that is, had to hold my hand until we reached safety. At least today I had no worries our foes might eat me." Dora tossed her head back and laughed.

For the third time that day, or perhaps even the fourth or fifth—he'd lost count along the way—Rex found himself at a loss for words. When he regained control over his tongue, he sallied on. "Be that as it may, I'd never forgive myself if something happened to you. I'll ask Mrs Meyrick to arrange for someone to drive you home once it gets dark. I'll go to the police. No matter what they say about Freddie's case, they can hardly turn a blind eye to a shooting in Belgravia."

"Can't they?" Dora countered. "Two weeks ago, I wager you'd have said they wouldn't ignore the death of a dear friend of a peer of the realm. And yet, Freddie's case was closed, unsolved. My faith in your Yard dwindles with each passing moment. I'm sure you'll understand if I struggle to take comfort in their abilities to keep me safe."

"I'll protect you."

"Like you did today?" Dora softened her voice. "I have a personal rule to not volunteer for target practice more than once a month. My quota has been met, and then some. The police have little incentive to step up their efforts. Who will clamour on behalf of a simple girl like me?"

Theodora Laurent hardly met the description of a simple girl, but Rex got her meaning. He hurried to put her mind at ease. "I'll not rest until this is solved. In the meantime, I have a house in the country. You could go there. Take your companion with you. You'll be safe."

"And leave the few friends I have? I intend for London to be my home. Running for the hills after a month hardly bodes well."

"Brighton? Bath? You could enjoy the waters," Rex offered, although he knew he was grasping at straws. He was powerless to stop himself. His family had drilled into him the responsibilities of a gentleman.

"Boring!" Dora shook her head, sending her hair waving. "A dip in the sea would wash the colour right out of my life. I need freedom, Lord Rex. I want to float on the dulcet tones of the latest American jazz singer and shake my hips to the wail of the trumpet."

As if to prove her point, Dora rose from her chair and sashayed away from the table. She danced and jived to music only she could hear. Male and female workers in the club alike interrupted their work to view her in awe.

Rex had to put a stop to this nonsense before someone got killed. He slammed his fist against the table with a rattle of glass and china. Dora halted mid-step and spun around, her doe eyes wide.

"Be serious, Theodora," he growled, using her first name without a second thought. "Someone sees you as a risk. I can only assume that this person has reason to believe you know something of value. Unless you've been involved with more people than Freddie, that is."

Dora propped her hands on her hips and glowered down her nose at him. "Freddie and I were having fun, and I did not need to look elsewhere for entertainment. I've already told you I'm hiding no truths or evidence. I'll swear on the bible if I must. For all we know, you were the one sitting in the sights."

"Me?" Rex reared back. That hadn't crossed his mind. His brow wrinkled in concentration as he weighed the possibility. He plumbed the depths of his memory, but nothing new came to light.

Dora stalked closer. Ignoring her chair, she pushed the tray of half-eaten sandwiches to the side and perched on the edge of the table, dangerously near. Then she leaned over so that their noses were almost touching.

"What if you were the target, Rexy-poo? Would you still be so eager to turn everything over to an investigator and hope for the best? To hide yourself away from the world until someone with no stake in the game gives you clearance to emerge?"

Rex gulped. "Err, nooo..."

Dora's lips curled into a smirk. "I thought not." She straightened up and leapt to her feet, once again giving him room to breathe. "This room is becoming claustrophobic. Already, I can feel my world shrinking. There has to be another solution, one which will suit both of us, but we'll never come up with it here. Grab your glass and the bottles and we'll take this show on the road."

Dora picked up her wrap, hat, and handbag and waltzed off with nary a backward glance.

"Go where? And how?" Rex argued as he raced to keep up. "We haven't got a car."

Dora glanced over her shoulder. "Of course we do. I agree that the dismal ride we borrowed from your warehouse lacks glamour, but it has four wheels and an engine. Don't forget the drinks."

Rex grabbed the bottles of gin and tonic and tucked them under his arm without asking himself why he was following her orders. He called out, "It isn't safe. What if he, they, whoever they are, sees us again?"

Dora's tinkling laugh filled the empty room. "Oh Rex darling, aren't you a laugh? Sitting in that boring excuse for a car, even my mother wouldn't recognise me."

Rex hurried to catch up, having no idea how honest Dora had been. Not a month earlier, while staying at the Grosvenor, Dora had crossed paths with her mother in the grand hotel lobby. She'd hardly dared to draw a breath for fear of attracting her attention.

She needn't have worried. The last time her mother had laid eyes on her, she'd been a young girl with her hair in braids and dirt smudges on her cheeks. There was no reason whatsoever for anyone to connect that image with the modern day temptress known as Theodora Laurent.

Her mother had sailed past, deep in conversation with a

friend, and none the wiser of her close encounter with her wayward child.

Rex was equally clueless as he followed Dora onto the pavement. The sun was shining. His eyes were open. But he'd be damned if he understood what he was seeing.

Chapter 6
Dora's bitter pill

"Drive anywhere," Dora instructed after Rex pulled away from the kerb.

"I should aim for the Victoria Embankment," he mumbled.

"Where, no doubt, our foes lie in wait for us to appear as if by magic. That is the last place we should go. Drive in circles, if you like, but don't go anywhere near the police."

Silence fell over the pair as the rhythm and motion of the busy city centre provided background music for their thoughts. Dora was grateful for the quiet. Despite her cavalier comments while in the empty club, she was also suffering from worry.

She'd experienced her share of danger over the years. It was part and parcel of life as a spy. This, however, felt somehow different. Someone had aimed a weapon at her. It hardly mattered if she'd been the target.

To make matters worse, there was no point in looking for the cavalry. She was it. Rex could holler and wail at the investigators at Scotland Yard all he wanted. They would not lift a finger, not so long as Lord Audley was calling the shots.

In his circumspect way, Audley had practically begged her to solve Freddie's murder. It had seemed a simple enough task, certainly far less risky than her normal line of work. But all that had changed when a bullet flew over her head.

Dora flicked a quick look at the man at her side. Rex had a deep furrow on his forehead and his hands were clenched tightly on the steering wheel. Why did it have to be him?

He may not know of their past connection, but Dora would never forget the events that had brought their lives together, passing like ships in the night. How could she, when the result had put her on the path that led to this very moment in time?

Outside their car, men hurried back and forth. Women chatted at tables outside cafes. The shop windows hinted at the abundance of goods inside. Other parts of town still bore the scars of the bombs from the Great War, but not here.

Dora and Rex kept their scars hidden from the world as well. Four years earlier, both were stationed in Le Touquet. Suffering and dying were par for the course, so close to the front lines. Yet, neither of them was prepared to see someone dear to them die, murdered at the hand of a traitor.

Lord Audley had given them each permission to investigate the crime. Rex worked the traditional routes while, unbeknownst to him, Dora operated in the shadows. Together, they'd seen justice served.

Perhaps therein lay the solution to Dora's problems. She had to solve Freddie's death. She knew Rex was unlikely to let the matter go.

She could move them both around like pieces on a chessboard. Only she would know of the existence of the hand. If she played the game right, Rex need never know the full extent of her involvement in the case.

Who knew? He might even be of assistance. Freddie's murder echoed like hoofbeats through their lives. She could use Rex to investigate for horses and leave herself free to worry about zebras.

Once again, her spirits rose. She knew she'd find a way out of their predicament. Getting Rex to play along would be no trouble at all. Step one was to eliminate the space between them.

Literally.

Dora slid across the bench seat and tucked against Rex's side. He tensed.

"I hope you don't mind... I feel safer sitting away from the window."

Rex nodded, but his shoulders remained tight. He smelled of sweat, soap, and sandalwood. When he flexed his fingers, Dora noted the ring finger on his right hand was crooked. She bet there was a story behind that injury.

"Do you mind if I call you Rex? After everything we've experienced today, referring to you as your lordship seems odd. And you must call me Theodora."

"Very well," Rex agreed.

Slowly but surely, Dora chipped away at Rex's granite facade. She asked about his finger, told a story from her own childhood, and eventually worked her way back to their current situation.

"Tell me, Rex. Why did you come to my house this morning? I know you wanted me to go to the police, but what if they'd ignored us? Would you have let it go?"

Dora glanced up in time to see Rex's face flush. "You'll think me foolish, but I planned to look into Freddie's death. On my own, that is."

"Why would I think you are foolish?" Dora cried. "I wish I'd thought of it myself. Right now, it is as if we're the only two people in the world who care to know the truth. Who else is dedicated enough to see this through to the end?"

Rex kept his gaze fixed on the road. "No one, I fear."

Dora wrapped her fingers around Rex's arm, silently asking

for his attention. He guided the car into a space on the side of the road.

"We have to do this, don't you see? Freddie's gone, and we're left. Someone sees us as a threat. The only way we'll ever be clear of this burden is if we find out who is behind it all."

Rex's jaw clenched, making the muscle in his jaw tick. "I'll do it... it's my responsibility."

"No," Dora said. "We make a good team. You saw that today. Plus, there's safety in numbers. If one of us leaves the other behind, we'll only cause a distraction. You can stay with me. I've plenty of room."

Rex paled. "I don't... err, that is. Well, people would talk, Theodora. About the two of us."

Dora shrugged aside his concern. "That's half the fun, darling."

Rex flushed and tugged at the collar of his shirt. "Be that as it may, what would society think of me taking up with you, with Freddie barely in the grave? My grandmother would have words for me."

Dora was nonplussed. She'd been so sure he'd fall neatly into her trap. She gritted her teeth. Only one thing left.

"Then I'll stay with you. Incognito, if you will," she hastened to add. "I've plenty of experience slipping out the side door. Can your servants keep a secret?"

"Can anyone's?"

"Mine can," Dora answered. "Surely, if you told them it was a matter of life or death, they'd remain mum. We'd keep separate rooms, of course. All above board. We'll give them no reason to talk."

Rex fiddled with this collar. Dora was so close to getting her way. All he needed was a tiny nudge to get over the line.

"Do it for Freddie, Rex. Your dear, dear friend."

It was a dreadful card to play, but Dora had no regrets. As

Lyly wrote, the rules of fair play don't apply in matters of love and war. He'd meant a different sort of matters of the heart, but the logic behind his poetic line remained.

"Fine, but please, Theodora, you must be on your absolute best behaviour."

Dora was so busy congratulating herself she failed to question why he was so insistent that she play the role of good society girl. It wasn't until he turned the car into the drive at the rear of a house in Mayfair that she thought to ask whether he lived alone.

"This is my grandmother's home."

Dora fought the urge to throw herself from the car and run screaming in the other direction. "Which grandmother?" she inquired, amazed at how steady her voice was.

"The Dowager Duchess of Rockingham. On my father's side."

Dora clenched her teeth to keep from groaning aloud. If there were odes written proclaiming Dora's beauty, poems about the dowager were more likely to be battle cries. To say she had a reputation of being a battle axe was like calling the sinking of the Titanic a minor incident.

Why couldn't his granny have been some doddering old fool of a woman, half blind and deaf to boot?

Dora tamped her emotions down and forced herself to see the upside. If she hoped to have any relationship with her family, she'd have to fool people like Rex's grandmother. Far better to assess her capabilities now than after she'd contacted her parents.

Her prolonged silence amused Rex. "There's still the option of the old pile in the countryside. It's sitting empty."

"No, no. That's unnecessary." Turnabout was a bitter pill, but Dora swallowed it nonetheless. "With her playing chaperone, there will be no doubts as to the state of your virtue.

I suppose you should explain the situation to her before you make my presence known. Hand me your coat. I'll keep it over my head until we get inside. If you have a phone I can use, I'll call my companion while you speak with your grandmother."

Rex parked the car outside the mews and shrugged off his coat. He passed it over and then exited.

Dora didn't wait for him to open her door. She slid across and followed him out, sticking close to him. With his jacket covering her head, she couldn't see more than a yard on either side. Still, she kept to a measured gait, adopting a cadence more appropriate for a servant than the upper class. From a distance, the brown of her dress might almost be mistaken for the uniform of a lady's maid.

Rex kept a tight hold of her hand until they reached a doorway. When they were inside, Rex gave her the okay to drop her disguise.

While Rex shrugged his clothing back into place, Dora took the opportunity to stare unabashedly at her surroundings. He'd led her into the library. Rows and rows of shelves lined the walls, filled with books in gold-stamped leather bindings. To her left was a window seat lined with cushions and a view of the garden. To her right sat a heavy mahogany desk.

"Make yourself at home," Rex insisted. "I'll station a footman outside to ensure no one comes in until we're ready. The telephone is on the credenza by the door."

Dora assured him she'd be fine, and he left without a backwards glance.

First things first. Dora picked up the phone and requested the operator connect her to her home. After several rings, Inga answered.

"You'll never guess where I am," Dora said by way of introduction.

"I don't believe the phone lines reach heaven or hell yet, so

I'll start by guessing you're still wandering the Earth. Based on your gleeful tone, it must be the last place that would come to my mind. Therefore, I'll discard my guess of the 43 and opt for the home of Lord Rex. How did I do?"

"Splendid, as always," Dora answered, not at all displeased with her friend's nimble mind. She'd have been disappointed if Inga hadn't come up with the right answer in short order. "There's an unexpected twist to my tale, Inga dear. I'm temporarily relocating my residence to Mayfair. I need you to pack a suitcase with *the necessities* and come keep me company. Have Harris bring you around to the rear entrance." She waited until Inga located a pencil before adding the exact address.

"I suppose you'll need clothing for *all occasions*, will you not?"

"Indeed! You've understood the situation precisely. It may take me a short while to get settled. Shall we aim for you to arrive a little before the dinner bell?"

"I'll inform Harris of the plans and see you then." Inga ended the call without saying goodbye. It was a habit formed of necessity. When operating undercover, goodbye felt awfully final.

Dora replaced the receiver and tiptoed to the door. She leaned her head against it, but couldn't hear a sound coming from the corridor outside. Rex had said to make herself at home. If she were in the comfort of her parlour, she'd be busy researching Rex's family. While she obviously knew who he was, she hadn't thought of him in years. She needed to fill the gaps in his familial structure and position in society.

With a practiced eye, she skimmed the shelves until she spotted a familiar volume. Like all upper crust families, the home of the Dowager Duchess of Rockingham held a copy of Debrett's. Dora slid it from the shelf, noting the lack of dust along the top. No one's housekeeping staff was that efficient.

More likely than not, the dowager often used it for her own reference.

The alphabetical order facilitated Dora's search. Within moments, she confirmed Rex was indeed the second son of the family. All the wealth with none of the responsibility — an ideal position, if you were lucky enough to get it.

Although Dora's real identity merited a line of mention in the venerable tome, Theodora Laurent was nowhere to be found. Her history was recorded elsewhere. That was fine with Dora. Glory came in many shapes and sizes. She'd long ago determined she wanted to be known for her acts rather than her place of birth.

Dora closed the book and slid it back into place. It was no time to be maudlin or wander down memory lane. There were appearances to keep and mysteries to unfold. Rest was rare and to be treasured. She returned to her wanderings around the room until the contents of a low shelf caught her eye. Her eyes lit up with delight.

When Rex returned half an hour later, he found her curled on the sofa reading Conan Doyle's The Hound of the Baskervilles, while the cat snoozed near her feet. Had he been wise to her games, he'd have no doubt understood the irony of her choice.

Alas, he was not. Death and rebirth were the furthest things from his mind when he laid eyes on the gorgeous creature known as Theodora Laurent.

Rex cleared his throat to get her attention. "Grandmama would like to meet you." He stood stock still while Dora searched his face. With a reassuring smile, he encouraged her to mark her place in the book.

"It's no matter," she replied. "I've read it so many times that I simply flip to a page and begin wherever I land." Dora set the book on a table, and murmured an apology for disturbing the cat. "Has he got a name?"

"Mews," Rex answered, blushing ever so slightly. He scratched his nose. "My grandmama's cat. She found him in the mews behind the house."

"Thanks for keeping me company, Mews." Dora scratched the cat's chin. She kept half an eye on Rex and noted him scratching his nose for a second time. "Are you allergic to the cat?"

"Err, yes," Rex backed away from the animal, giving a good show, and scratched his nose a third time.

More likely that Rex was allergic to the truth. Dora had immediately recognised the cat, even though it had been a tiny kitten the last time she'd seen it, some four years earlier. It had been during their time at the front.

Unbeknownst to Rex, Dora had crept into his room and left him an anonymous tip. While there, she'd encountered the kitten. Whether Rex had found him in the wartime stables, she couldn't say. However, she had a strong suspicion that the cat's name had more to do with its attempts to miaow than with its birthplace. When she'd crept into the room, the little beast had beckoned her to play with a series of plaintive mews.

Meeting the cat a second time had brought an unexpected gift. Lord Rex had a tell. Dora now knew to examine his words carefully if he scratched his nose while saying them. She smiled in pure pleasure, smoothed her skirts, and told Rex to lead the way.

Chapter 7
Rex's grandmother

Rex guided her down the corridor to where his grandmother waited in the drawing room. What did Theodora make of the house? He had a difficult time believing the richness of her surroundings might overwhelm her. Still, how familiar was she with antiques and artwork? Perhaps her cool demeanour came from a lack of awareness. He conceded it was possible she knew little of the value of the landscapes and portraits hanging on the wall.

Rex promised himself he'd be an excellent host. It fell to him to make sure she felt comfortable during her stay. After all, like him, she was in a state of mourning over the loss of a friend.

Before he opened the door to the drawing room, he paused his steps and faced Dora. "I'll stay by your side."

Dora flashed him a cheeky smile and patted him on the shoulder. "Chased by a lion. Remember, darling? I'm hardly the type to tremble in the face of a challenge. Besides, everyone loves Theodora Laurent. Even her enemies."

With that, Dora used her hip to bump him aside, twisted the knob, and preceded him into the room.

The dowager duchess sat like a queen on a throne waiting to

hear from supplicants. She was in her usual position, seated in a velvet upholstered armchair near the fireplace. A portrait of her in her younger years hung in a place of honour above the mantle.

Both in the portrait and in real life, she dripped with jewels and gold. Her dress was made of the finest materials and cut in a style popular at the turn of the century. Her face was impassive as the pair crossed the room.

Dora stopped at the edge of the Aubusson carpet and graced the dowager with a warm smile. "Lady Rockingham, it is a pleasure to make your acquaintance. I apologise for my unexpected arrival. I'd have awaited an invitation, but I think we both recognise such a thing wouldn't be possible."

"No, I should think not," Rex's grandmother agreed. Her chin rose a notch as she examined Dora from head to toe.

Rex could only hope that it was a sign of improvement in her estimation of Theodora. She'd been none too pleased to hear that one of London's more notorious occupants was currently sitting in her library. Her displeasure had deepened upon learning the stay was to be extended, end date unknown. Only him explaining it was a matter of life or death had prevented his grandmother from showing Theodora back out the way she came in.

Despite his grandmama's dispassionate gaze, Theodora stood tall. Few women of the Ton dared to look the dowager in the eye. For this woman, of all people, to show such strength of character and confidence came as a complete shock to both Rex and the dowager.

Rex rushed to diffuse the tension. "Why don't you have a seat, Theodora?" He motioned to the sofa nearest his grandmother's chair.

Dora ignored him. Her attention never wavered from the

lady of the house. "Since this isn't a social visit, I propose we set the niceties aside and speak plainly."

The dowager narrowed her gaze, but remained silent. Dora took that as permission to continue.

"The rules of polite society dictate that women such as ourselves should forever remain in separate social circles. Here, in the privacy of your home, we have two options. First, we can conform to these dictates. Lord Rex and I can exit to another room, the library or the study, for example, while you retain full usage of your normal areas of the house."

"Theodora," Rex whispered, making a desperate attempt to intervene in what he saw as a terrible mistake. What was she doing?

His grandmama wanted to know as well. "And the second option?"

"Naturally, the second option is my preference, but I'm willing to follow your lead. Since no one is the wiser, we could throw such nonsensical edicts aside and get to know one another. I may be young, but I'm well-travelled and have had extensive interactions at the highest levels of polite society. From what I've heard of your reputation, you have shown regard for those with high intellect and interesting stories. I believe, given the time, I can demonstrate these characteristics."

Rex held his breath. He didn't know whether to bodily throw himself between the women or sink deeper into the background. There was no risk of fisticuffs, but his grandmother's displeasure had burned many a man and woman over the years. It had likely been decades since someone spoke so openly and honestly.

The women held each other's gazes, neither backing down, each taking the other's measure.

To Rex's surprise, it was his grandmother who broke first.

"Miss Laurent, many a woman of your ilk has sashayed through London over the years. Until you walked into my drawing room, I presumed you were like the rest of them. In this particular case, I'm delighted to be proven wrong. Please, make yourself comfortable and let's see if we can't find a common ground."

If that weren't enough to send Rex's head spinning, the saucy wink Dora gave him when her back was to his grandmother sent him right over the edge. He flopped into a nearby chair and pinched his hand. The pain assured him he was awake. Perhaps he'd somehow stumbled into an alternate universe.

It took some time before he was able to wrap his head around the scene before him. Who would believe him if he spoke of seeing his stalwart grandmama engaging in conversation with a single woman of questionable background and few morals?

And what a conversation it was!

"Are you familiar with the works of D H Lawrence?" the dowager asked.

"Of course. I had lunch with David and Frieda in a small, beachside cafe near Taormina last summer. We enjoyed the most divine aragosta and gorged ourselves on grilled swordfish rolls. Somewhere on my bookshelves at home, I have an autographed copy of *Sons and Lovers*. I must admit, however, that I prefer Wharton's *Age of Innocence*."

"The tale of a man who spends his whole life wanting the femme fatale, only to walk away from her at the end? You would!" The dowager laughed so long and hard that Rex half feared for her heart. "Dear girl, what I wouldn't give to spend a moment walking in your shoes! Just a short one, mind you."

"As Ms Wharton so elegantly conveyed, the ideal of the carefree existence is greater than the reality. I daresay you'd be disappointed by the many hours I spend each day on mundane tasks. Speaking of the mundane, if it isn't too much trouble, I'd like my companion, Miss Kay, to join us. Everyone knows she's my dearest friend. If someone is after me, they might well take action against her to compel my cooperation."

The dowager acquiesced to her request. "In for a penny, in for a pound."

"Excellent. She should be here soon with our bags."

"Rex, be a good lad and let Sheffield know he needs to make arrangements for our guests," the dowager said. "He'll need to have a strict word with the staff if we're to keep this quiet. Tell him to do whatever is necessary."

Rex did as bade, although he was still half-convinced he was living a fever-dream and not firmly planted in the real world. He stepped into the study and rang for Sheffield to join him.

"Did you require something, my lord?" Sheffield asked when he arrived a moment later.

The butler was the picture of quiet dignity in his perfectly pressed black suit, sedate grey waistcoat, white shirt, and black tie. His white hair was oiled into place. The only wrinkles were those on his face.

Sheffield had worked for Rex's grandmother for as long as he could remember. He'd seen Rex grow from a young boy sliding down the bannister into a man grown too fast when forced to reckon with the realities of war. Never once had Rex's antics thrown the man. Somehow, that knowledge wasn't reassuring at this particular moment.

"We have a guest. Well, two actually."

"Very good, sir."

"They'll be staying with us indefinitely."

"Understood. I'll ask the maids to make up the rose room and the blue room, and to set extra places at dinner. Will there be anything else?"

Rex wiped his palms on his trousers and wished for once

Sheffield would act like a normal man and show a hint of curiosity. Was it too much to hope the butler would ask for the names of their guests?

Apparently, it was.

Sheffield stared straight ahead, awaiting further orders.

"Grandmama has absolute faith in your discretion," Rex began. He stopped mid-sentence when he caught sight of a flush climbing up the butler's neck.

Rex replayed the last few seconds in his mind. He'd meant well, but in retrospect, his hesitancy to blurt out the truth of the situation had made it sound the opposite of what he intended.

"I think it's better if I come right out and tell you what is going on. Our house guest is Theodora Laurent."

Sheffield's eyes bulged out of his sockets, but he otherwise remained silent.

"Her companion will be here shortly with their bags. I've asked the pair of them to help me look into Freddie's death."

"And they need to come here to do that?" Sheffield's displeasure was evident in his horrified tone.

"They are already here, or at least one of them, anyway. Their lives are in danger, and we're offering them a safe place to hide. To avoid raising eyebrows, I escorted Miss Laurent in through the rear entrance. She's in the drawing room with Grandmama."

"Well, I never!" Sheffield caught himself before he could further chastise his employer. His glower, however, did an excellent job of communicating his disapproval of the young master.

Rex found himself on the defensive. It didn't matter that he didn't owe the butler an explanation for his behaviour. Sheffield was his grandmother's right-hand man. He'd turned a blind eye many a time when Rex's childish acts stretched beyond the confines of the nursery. To have made it this far

before losing Sheffield's high regard, only to lose it now —
when his acts were purely charitable — was enough to sour
Rex's stomach.

"Grandmama asked me to leave them. I know you'll find
this hard to believe, but the pair were, I daresay, getting along
swimmingly. In fact, if I were to return now, I'm sure
Grandmama would find some other pretence for removing me
from the room."

"I see." Sheffield's expression made it clear he didn't see.
Nonetheless, he remembered his place and ended the
discussion there. "I believe I understand the matter perfectly,
your lordship. I'll have a word with the staff. Consider their lips
sealed."

Rex breathed an audible sigh of relief. "Thank you,
Sheffield. That will be all."

After the butler's departure, Rex found himself alone in the
spacious library. The books would tell no tales. He flopped onto
the leather sofa and loosened his tie. With his eyes closed and
head resting against the back of the seat, he tried to imagine the
scene in the drawing room. What could the pair be discussing
now?

The more he pondered the matter, the more
discombobulated he became. Two more wildly different
women, Rex had never seen. Yet, they'd had no trouble finding
common ground. What did that say about Theodora?

What did that say about his grandmother?

Rex bottled that thought and dropped it into the darkest
depths of his memory, never to consider again. "I need a drink,"
he announced to the empty room.

He poured himself a healthy measure of fine brandy, raised
a silent toast to Freddie, and tossed it back. The book-lined walls
kept him company. It was far from the first time he'd found
solitude in the written word. After another measure of brandy,

this time sipped more slowly, an old quote by one of his favourite authors rose from his memories.

'Courage is resistance to fear, mastery of fear—not absence of fear,' Mark Twain had once said.

Rex had fear enough to get him through the coming days. Between now and dinner time, he'd better find a way to master it.

Chapter 8
The doctored drink

After a dinner of chilled soup with smoked salmon, ham hock terrine with roasted parsnips, and a slow-roasted brisket served with generous portions of potatoes dauphinoise, Dora knew she should decline the offer of dessert. One look at the delicate French tarts dusted with sparkling sugar proved the futility of any thoughts of her waistline. It took all her years of etiquette lessons to keep from eating the dessert in two extra-large bites.

The dinner conversation had proven to be equally delightful. With the four of them — herself, Rex, Inga, and Lady Rockingham — clustered around one end of the long dining table, the talk had flowed as smoothly as the wine. They'd touched on fashion, film, the latest exhibit at the National Gallery, and dipped a toe in the controversial topic of politics.

In each case, Dora and Inga had held their own, never failing to show an opinion. They'd agreed on their strategy in hurried whispers while dressing for dinner. The dowager was known for her forthrightness, and would certainly frown upon any dithering or straddling of the middle ground. Although their stay at Rockingham house would remain a secret from the rest of the world, the dowager would remember them.

Dora had long ago learned to store potential allies in her pockets. Some days she felt like a magpie as she gathered rumours and facts in equal measure, weaving them into the fabric of her memory. She couldn't risk being caught off guard by a chance encounter. Her usefulness to the realm was as much due to the assignments she completed as her ability to assemble insights into a big picture view.

Despite the success of dinner, at times, Dora suspected Rex was testing her. She'd seen the behaviour before. Men didn't know what to make of females who held opinions, and even less what to do with those who dared to voice them. With Inga's careful assistance, Dora had walked a tightrope. She'd displayed just enough of her personality to appeal to the dowager, balanced with hints of weakness to keep Rex wrapped around her finger.

Dora moaned with pleasure as the flaky pastry melted in her mouth, covering the sigh of relief that dinner was nearly done. When the plates were scraped clear, the dowager declared it time to retire.

"I can't remember the last time I enjoyed such a scintillating evening. I'm aware you young people have much to discuss, so I'll wish you a good night and leave you in peace."

"Oh?" Inga asked. "I thought you might join me in a hand of whist. If it's too much, I'll understand."

"Won't you need to discuss the, ahem, matter with Miss Laurent and my grandson?"

"Miss Kay usually made herself scarce when Freddie came around," Dora explained.

"By all means, she's more than welcome to keep me company." The dowager rose from her chair with Inga following suit. On their way out the door, the dowager said,

"Whist is so acceptable. What say you to a less traditional game?"

"Poker? Blackjack? I should warn you," Inga replied, "after our visit to Texas, I am very proficient at bluffing."

"Really?" The dowager didn't sound in the least upset with this news.

Dora half-wished she could be a fly on the wall for the remainder of their evening. There'd be time enough for fun once her work was complete. She turned her half-lidded gaze to the man sitting across from her and tried not to laugh when he blushed. "Shall we excuse ourselves to the library?"

"What? Oh yes, of course."

Dora glided over with the grace of a dancer and joined Rex at the head of the table. Without waiting for an invitation, she slid her arm through his. "Lead away, darling. Wherever you go, I'll follow."

Rex gulped and fixed his eyes firmly ahead, not daring to even chance a glimpse of the alluring creature at his side.

Dora kept a tight hold on Rex even after they were behind the closed door of the library. She angled him toward the sofa and offered to pour them both a nightcap.

"But you're the guest," he protested.

"It's naught but a little thing," she replied. "Consider it a thank you for being such an excellent host to myself and my companion. Other men wouldn't have been nearly as kind-hearted."

While she chattered, she poured a splash of Port into the Baccarat crystal glasses. With her back to him, she twisted the ruby setting on her bracelet and tipped a dark powder into one of the glasses. A quick swirl and the powder disappeared.

Tasteless, odourless, and completely harmless, the powder posed no real threat to Rex. He'd remember the evening, left only to wonder why he'd been so forthcoming to her questions.

Come morning, he'd chalk it up to the spirits and her charms, none the wiser to the chemical aid that had loosened his tongue and lowered his inhibitions.

"Here you are, Rex." Dora sat beside him on the sofa, angling so she could face him. "Shall we raise our glasses in a toast? To Freddie!"

"To Freddie," Rex agreed. He drank a deep swallow of the maroon liquid, taking a moment to savour the taste.

Dora made another toast to Rex's grandmother, and finally one to the two of them. By the time she was done, both glasses were in need of a top up, exactly as she'd intended. She let Rex take care of the task, basking in the languid state that followed a long day and lengthy dinner. Her shoes fell from her feet and she pulled her knees up, further sinking into the deep cushions nestled in the corner.

Rex passed her a glass and returned to his seat next to her. He cast a glance at her relaxed position and followed her cue, loosening his tie and crossing his feet at the ankles. The only lighting came from a pair of table lamps on either end of the sofa. With the rest of the room in shadows, and the servants out of earshot, the world shrank until Dora and Rex were its only occupants.

"Tell me about Freddie, about your younger days."

Rex got that faraway look in his eyes as he waltzed along memory lane. "I met Freddie on my second day at Eton. A few of the older boys decided to knock the spirit out of me. You know how boys can be."

"Freddie leapt in and stopped them?"

"Ha! Not exactly. He and I were the same age. He stepped into the circle and put his back against mine. Said they'd have to take on both of us... which they promptly did, pummelling us into the ground. We spent a day in the infirmary and that was it. Blood brothers for life."

"That story doesn't surprise me in the least," Dora said, without needing to lie. "Freddie learned of my arrival in London through a shared acquaintance and rushed over to introduce himself. He promised to squire me around town and present me to everyone who was anyone."

"And here I thought he'd simply succumbed to your charms!"

"He did, but not until day two," Dora retorted, coaxing a laugh from Rex. "The world is certainly dimmer without his giving spirit to light our lives."

"Indeed." Rex sipped his drink and stared off into space.

Dora waited patiently for him to speak again. The silence stretched longer and longer until she worried he was growing morose. "Penny for your thoughts..."

Rex startled at the sound of her voice, as though he'd forgotten she was there. "I'm being a terrible host."

"Not at all," Dora rushed to reassure him. "Were you thinking about another memory from your days with Freddie?"

Rex shook his head. "I wish I could remember more of the good right now, but I'm mired in questions of why he died. Why was Freddie in that godawful place? He wasn't the type to take risks simply for the excitement. He had to have been there for a reason."

"You think he might have been meeting someone? Wouldn't he have told you? Or me, for that matter?" Dora was desperate to uncover what Rex thought.

"Honestly, the only answer that comes to my mind is that he met someone there because they asked for help. He'd have kept such a request a secret. Freddie wasn't one to toot his own horn. He was perfectly content with most of the world seeing him as little more than another frivolous man of wealth gadding about the society pages."

Dora pressed Rex harder. She was convinced that

somewhere in his memories of Freddie, she'd find a clue. "Surely if someone was in danger, Freddie would have told someone. Did he do anything unusual in the days leading up to his death? Was he seen anywhere? Spotted speaking to someone?"

"Not that I am aware," Rex growled in frustration. "I was away from town the week prior to his death. I made it back in time to read of the murder in the papers. If only he'd waited for my return. Surely, he must have known I'd have lent a hand with whatever he was doing. But that was just like him to help someone with chasing glory."

"What do you mean?" Dora took Rex's hands in hers, begging him to reveal his secrets. The physical touch combined with the inhibition-lowering drug worked like magic. "Who would come to Freddie for help?"

"A member of his staff?" Rex glanced upwards as he searched his mind. "One of the men from the war? I'm sure he kept in touch with a few of them. Still, I can't see any of those people demanding a meeting in the slums. Can you?"

Dora shook her head, agreeing with his assessment. No one who knew the young dandy and thought highly of him would drag him to such a location.

Rex was still talking. "It was such a strange choice of a meeting point. Why would Freddie feel comfortable venturing into such a spot? He must have had some guarantee of his safety."

"Perhaps..."

"Or... maybe he knew the owner!" Rex sat up straight, electrified by his thoughts. "Why, this is something I hadn't conceived. What if Freddie had paid the owner to keep an eye on him? The owner had to have seen something!"

Dora had to admit she liked the direction of Rex's thoughts, but the strange glint in his eye had her worried.

The cat emerged from behind the sofa, wandering past and issuing a plaintive yowl. It went to the glass doors that opened to the garden and stared upward at the door handle. One didn't need to speak cat in order to understand the request.

Rex was still muttering under his breath when he rose from the sofa to do the cat's bidding. He leaned over and stroked the cat's head before opening the door.

Allergy, indeed. Dora stifled a chuckle. Rex would make a terrible spy if he couldn't stick to his cover of lies for even a day.

Rex was slow to close the door. The night air had a crisp edge, but wasn't cold. From where she sat, Dora could see the brightest stars twinkling through the haze that perpetually hung over the city. In the countryside, thousands of stars shone down upon the occupants of England's rolling hills. Here, they were lucky to see three or four.

It was the perfect night for assignations. A long coat, flipped up collar, and a cap would be disguise enough. No one would question why a man walked the streets after hours, not when the weather was this fine.

Rex must have had the same thought. He turned around and fixed his gaze on Dora, his eyes bright with excitement. "I must go to the pub—the Ten Bells. Tonight... right now! The trail may already be cold. I have to speak with the owner and any regulars. Someone will remember seeing something!"

Dora reared back in horror. "No, Rex! The police will have already questioned everyone."

Rex sneered in disdain. "The police were lucky to get the location of his body from the residents of Spitalfields. I doubt they bothered asking anything."

"Then we'll pay someone — an investigator..."

"That will take too long!" Rex loosened his tie and shrugged off his jacket. "I'll need to borrow clothing from one of the servants."

Dora bit back a scream of frustration. The last thing she needed was a pretty boy like Rex wandering around a cutthroat neighbourhood, asking questions. Assuming they didn't pick his pockets the moment he set foot into the area, he'd out himself at the first word from his posh mouth. Hiding the silver spoon took years of practice, a fact Dora had learned the hard way.

Fuelled by the concoction she'd used to lace his drink, Rex would be nearly impossible to stop. Short of disrobing and throwing herself on him, she'd never be able to talk him out of his dangerous plan. Given his single-minded focus, she feared even her bared breast wouldn't be enough.

She had no one to blame but herself. Therefore, she knew what she had to do.

"I'm coming with you. Don't argue," she hastened to add, holding up a hand to ward him off. She looked him dead in the eye and lied like the devil she was. "I grew up in a place like Spitalfields. If you plan to make it out with your head still attached to the rest of your body, you'll need my street smarts to keep you safe."

Chapter 9
They visit the Ten Bells

The taxi dropped the pair off at Liverpool Street Station. From there, it was a ten-minute walk to their actual destination. Not short enough for Rex's tastes. He grimaced with every step. The too-tight shoes on loan from his valet pinched his toes and rubbed at his heels. When they passed under a street lamp, Rex found himself once again staring in amazement at his companion's transformation.

Was it barely more than an hour earlier that he'd seen her reclining on his sofa with a glass of Port in her hand? He could find no sign of that lady of leisure in her now.

Dora's easy gait was gone, replaced by a weary trudge emphasised by the slump of her shoulders. He marvelled at her abilities. Her smooth pin curls were now a snarled mess peeking from under the brim of her simple hat. Her coat, dress, and shoes fit properly, but they were shabby and stained. He didn't ask where she'd got them.

The men and women walking past didn't give her a second glance. She faded into the background, one more poor soul with the weight of the world on her shoulders.

Who was the real Theodora?

The woman he'd dined with hadn't given even a hint of her meagre upbringing. She'd held her own through every twist and turn of the conversation. No matter how much he searched his recollections, he couldn't find a single memory of a mistake she'd made. Rumour claimed she'd always lived in the lap of luxury, and he'd had no trouble believing it.

Seeing her now, however...

How long must she have worked to smooth the rough edges of her vowels and her manners? Rex wanted to be angry with her for playing them all the fool. But how could he resent someone who'd risen from the slums to soar above the highest peaks of society?

He risked a glance, taking in the low-quality goods in the storefronts and the rough-dressed individuals walking along the pavement. He was bound to make some mistake and reveal his identity. Fear caused his feet to move faster. This outing was a terrible folly. What could he say when it had been his idea?

Dora reached over and grabbed his hand, threading her fingers between his. "Slow down," she whispered. "Most of the men and women here spent the bulk of their day labouring in a factory or down at the docks. They're far too tired to quick-step their way home."

Rex fought the urge to rush and slowed his gait.

"Excellent. Now, roll your shoulders forward and fix your gaze a half-step in front of you. Let me worry about finding the address." Dora squeezed Rex's hand in encouragement. "We've got another five minutes or so. How's your ability with accents? Any chance you performed Oliver Twist in school? Or even saw it at the West End?"

"I've read a Christmas Carol a time or two," Rex murmured. After a moment of thought, he twisted his mouth and said, "Please, sir, can you spare a shilling?"

"Egads, Rex, that was dreadful." Dora's snickers reached his ears, making him blush.

"Let's hear yours, then," he quipped.

Dora tossed him an affronted look. "All you dewdroppers in yer glad rags finkin' we're nothin' but dancin' monkeys fer yer entertainment!"

Rex goggled. Gone were all traces of the light French accent that coloured her English. She sounded exactly the same as the man who'd driven their taxi.

Dora gave him a bawdy wink. "What say we leave the conversation to me, old chap? You can nurse a pint while I hunt for someone who knows their onions, if you know what I mean."

Despite the chill of the May evening, Rex broke into a cold sweat that had nothing to do with their late night exercise. The last vestiges of the wine burned from his system, leaving behind a cool head and a heap of regret.

As much as he was loath to admit it, Rex was in over his head. He was so far down, he couldn't see even a glimpse of the sky above. He was ready to call a halt to the foolishness when Dora remarked they were on the right street.

"Should be the lit building up ahead," she muttered. "One last thing before we go in..."

Rex's head whipped to the side, and he stared at her in horror. What else could there be to say, and why was it so bad she'd waited until now to drop the other shoe?

"It's best for us both if the Bells' customers think we're together."

"We are together," he countered, not understanding.

"Together-together, darling," she purred, stepping so close that she rested her head on his shoulder. "Leer at my bubs a few times and hint we should take things upstairs. After that, you can leave it with me."

Rex stumbled to a halt outside the pub door. Dora rose onto

her toes and kissed his cheek, leaving a perfect lip shape behind. "For authenticity," she explained, and then opened the door and pulled him inside.

Rex half expected the pub to go silent at their arrival, but nary a head lifted to eye the newcomers. This wasn't the Ritz, where people came to see and be seen. People forgetting your face a few minutes after your arrival was part of the appeal of a back-alley slum pub.

Dora cut through the crowd like a hot knife and beelined for an empty table near the stairs to the upper floor. She motioned for Rex to take the chair in the corner. He expected her to sit across from him, but once again, she caught him off guard by plopping down in his lap instead.

Rex froze.

That was fine. Dora was in complete control of the situation.

She snaked his arm around her waist and nestled her nose into his neck, just below his ear. She whispered, her breath warm against his neck, "Slide you arm up and down my back and use the opportunity to survey the place." When he took too long to follow orders, she nibbled on his earlobe, shocking him back into action.

While pretending to sprinkle him with kisses, Dora kept up a steady stream of quiet instruction. Her no-nonsense tone helped him find his feet again. Gradually, he grew comfortable enough to look around.

The pub was a dimly lit, cramped space, with a low ceiling and a rough wooden floor. Walls once whitewashed now bore the stains of years of tobacco smoke and spilled beer. The only light came from a fireplace and a few lanterns hanging from the ceiling, casting shadows over the faces of the patrons.

Between the low ceiling and weak lighting, the interior was dark and full of shadows. Not far away, a group of rough-looking brawlers were trying their hand at darts, cheering and jeering one another in equal measure.

The mirror behind the bar was scratched and black with smoke, barely clean enough to reflect the bottles stacked against it. Serving at the bar were a man and woman, likely enough a married couple. The long hours and poor earnings had taken their toll on the pair, leaving them with stained clothing, missing teeth, and oily hair.

A fresh-faced barmaid sauntered over, cutting off his line of sight. "Canna get you two somethin'?"

Dora straightened up and fished a silver coin from between her cleavage. "Two pints of yer finest."

"How fine can the finest be in a place such as this?" Rex mumbled.

"No worse than the piss-poor drinks you indulged in during the war. Toss it back like a man and wipe your mouth on your sleeve. Do not ask for a napkin," she added, glaring him into submission.

"Here you are, miss." The barmaid placed two foaming mugs on the scarred table. She spun to leave, but Dora called her back.

"Got any rooms upstairs? Me old man and me are lookin' to have some fun. We've got money to pay."

"We've got a couple," the barmaid answered, sizing up the pair.

Dora knew they'd never withstand any serious scrutiny. She leapt to her feet, blocking the barmaid's view of Rex. "I'm not paying 'til I check 'em out. Last place had rats. Come on. Take me up."

Rex watched as Dora hustled the barmaid up the stairs. He wasn't alone in watching the women retreat. Every red-blooded man in the building paused to appreciate the sight of the trim legs and shapely rear ends disappearing upstairs.

One of the darts players whistled his appreciation. He placed his hands over his heart and mimed it beating out of his chest, earning a round of laughter from his mates.

"Which one are you claiming, Arnie?" Another man asked.

"Who said anything about sharing? I'm man enough to take them both. Not that they'd give the likes of you the time of day, Gord."

The man named Gord slammed his pint glass on the table and spread his arms wide, inviting his friend to say that again. "Yer wife wasn't complaining when I saw her last night, mate."

Rex sank lower in his chair and hid behind his glass. He doubted his few rounds of training with Ted 'Kid' Lewis at the National Sporting Club were of any use in a bar brawl. The roughnecks would hardly wait for a bell before throwing the first punch.

To his great relief, the two men burst into laughter and slapped each other on the back. Apparently, this sort of ribbing was part of their nightly entertainment.

Rex dared to straighten back up.

That was his mistake.

The movement caught Gord's eye.

"Eh, Arnie, get a load of the toff over there. He came in with the new girl."

Arnie shifted sideways until he could get a good luck of Rex. "That's no toff. Look at his duds. That coat's worse than mine."

Rex's heart was pounding. He gripped onto his glass like it was a life raft and sank deeper into the shadow of the staircase. He promised himself he'd keep his mouth shut, no matter what provocation the ruffians might offer.

Said ruffians, however, weren't on the same page. Gord squinted his eyes and sauntered closer, weaving a crooked path across the pub. "Stained duds don't fool me," he muttered. He stumbled right up to the edge of the table, slapped a hand on the top and leaned toward Rex. "Skin as smooth as a baby's arse. I told you 'e was a toff," he announced, swinging around to call to his friends. "Gents, we're in fine company tonight. Let's show Sir Toffington how we welcome the new clientele."

Rex barely had time to bark a word of protest before a pair of rough hands latched onto his arms and lifted him from his chair. Gord frogmarched him to the far side of the room, where his mates waited for his arrival.

Rex cast a desperate eye at the publican and his wife, fervently hoping for help. The publican grabbed a rag and went to work polishing the line of taps. His wife filled a glass of lager and leaned against the counter, ready for the show. It was more likely the King himself would make an appearance and save him than those two coming to his aid.

Gord guided him into a chair at their table and shoved it close, blocking any means of escape. "Don't worry, mate, we ain't gonna hurt ya. We'll win the clams off ya fair and square. What'll it be first? Cards? Dice?"

"Boxing?" Arnie piped up from the other side of the table. "Look at 'is hands, boys! Be a cryin' shame to bloody them after 'is valet put so much time and effort into filing 'is nails."

There were six of them now, big, burly men with broad shoulders, crooked noses, and burnt cheeks. They smelled of rotten seafood, sea air and sweat. Theodora had been right. These men spent their days slinging crates on the docks. Perhaps they even worked at a warehouse owned by his family.

Not that pointing that out now would do him any good. Rex didn't like his odds in a one-on-one match with any of these men, never mind taking on all six. He tossed a desperate glance at the stairs, praying he'd see Theodora making her way down.

The staircase was empty of everything but dust.

He was on his own, at least for a few more minutes. All he

had to do was survive. Surely Theodora would know how to get them out of this mess.

Calm blanketed his nerves. He was a smart enough gent. If he could survive weeks in the trenches with the huns lobbing poisonous gas canisters, hand bombs and bullets his way, day and night, then he could surely get through the next ten minutes.

But how to respond to their question? He'd hadn't a chance of denying their assessment of his social status. Therefore, his means of escape must lie with the truth.

Rex grabbed the deck of cards from the table and shuffled them with the ease of a pro. "Five-card draw. Starting bet is a shilling... unless that's too rich for your blood."

Arnie sank into the chair opposite and held out his hand. "Yer running the bank, mate. Anything you can afford is fine with the rest of us."

Rex smiled widely at the joke, despite it being at his expense, in every sense of the word.

Chapter 10
Rex's narrow escape

The upper floor of the pub was exactly as Dora expected it to be. A single narrow hallway ran down the back wall, with two doors leading off from it. The barmaid pulled a ring of keys from the front pocket of her apron and unlocked the door to the first.

"No rats, mice, nits or other vermin, as you can see. My parents don't allow anybody to run a business from up here, if you know what I mean." The young woman nodded at the rickety iron bed frame to emphasise her point. "Payment up front and we'll toss in a full English come morning. Me mum's blood pudding is famous around these parts. You won't be sorry."

Dora knew she'd be sorry if she spent a night on the lumpy mattress, or at least her back would. The whole room smelled heavily of bleach, but at least it was clean.

Dora closed the door and leaned against it, blocking any escape. She fished a couple of coins from her pocket and handed them to the maid. "This should cover the room. And this..." Dora hiked up her skirt until she could see the top of her stockings. From there, she retrieved a five-pound note. "This can be yours, if you can spare a few minutes."

"I ain't taking part in no sort of shenanigans, miss. Not even for a fiver."

"Pity that." Dora winked at the maid, further throwing her off balance. "Lucky for me, that isn't the kind of service I need. It's your memory I'm after, not your assets, considerable as they are."

The barmaid crossed her arms under her impressive breasts and gave Dora a deadpan stare. "I'm listening."

"A man died in the alley outside your pub. Did he come here often?"

The barmaid opened her mouth but shut it just as fast. She held out a hand and waited for Dora to hand over the note. "Just the once. He requested this room."

Interesting! Dora set aside her first impression and gave the interior a second inspection. There wasn't anything immediately apparent that would explain Freddie's interest in the place. "Who'd he make the arrangements with? You?"

"Aye, it was me. He caught me when I was carrying out the rubbish, offered me a few quid for letting him up the back stairs and into the room."

Satisfied that the barmaid wasn't going anywhere, Dora began a tour of the room. "Not that I'm ungrateful, but you're awfully forthcoming."

"The bloke's dead. You're here. Money's money."

In that, the young woman wasn't wrong. It might cost her another fiver, but Dora grew confident she'd get everything she needed from the girl.

"Why this room?"

"He didn't say."

Dora opened the window and gazed at the view. The room

looked out on the front street. All she could see was a weary old woman trudging past.

"I don't suppose you know why he chose that particular night."

"Funny thing, that." The barmaid held out a hand, waiting for another coin. The self-satisfied smirk on her face suggested she had plenty more to say, if the price was right.

Dora pulled up her skirt to reveal the other shapely leg and a second five-pound note. She pulled it free and then spun around in a circle, flashing her thighs. "The bank's run dry, so make this one last."

The maid had the gall to act affronted, but Dora caught her smiling when she thought Dora wasn't looking. She was probably already imagining the new summer wardrobe she could buy with ten quid.

"The other room is booked out by a regular." The maid thumbed a finger at the far wall. "Don't ask me his name because he ain't the type to leave a record. He came every Friday. Some of Arnie's mates from the docklands would turn up and disappear upstairs to meet with him. They always had plenty of funds for tips afterwards. Your friend, the dead man, requested use of this room on the last night either of 'em visited. He showed up just before nightfall, locked himself inside, and that was the last I saw of him. Alive, anyway. We heard a ruckus out back, a gunshot, and wisely decided to keep out of it."

Dora eyed the wall, making note of thick plaster surface. You might be able to listen in on the conversation next door, if the other guests talked loud enough. She couldn't imagine Freddie coming this far, only to catch a half-garbled conversation.

Dora retreated into the corner and tapped her chin. She was missing something, some trick. If Freddie timed his visit to overlap, he was either watching the comings and goings, or listening in on the meeting. In his shoes, she'd aim to do both. But how?

The furnishings offered little clue. Other than the bed, there was a single cupboard with a sagging door, and a washstand with an oval mirror hanging above it. On the far wall, there was nothing.

Well, not exactly nothing. Dora strode across the room and stood at an angle to the wall. From there, she could see a faint difference in the shade of paint and a single nail. Her gaze flicked back to the mirror. "Has that always hung there?"

"No. Used to hang on the other wall. When he came upstairs, the dead man asked if he could move it. Said something about fangs... fangs way? He went on and on about balance. I charged him an extra quid and told him to do whatever he liked."

"Feng Shui?" Dora highly doubted Freddie was employing the ancient Chinese arts in a room above a third rate pub. Frankly, she was even more surprised that Freddie knew such a thing existed. She crossed to the other side and gripped the edges of the mirror firmly. It was lighter than she expected. She had little trouble removing it from the nail. After sitting it on the bed for safekeeping, she turned back to see what was there.

A perfect circle, no more than a centimetre wide. It was the ideal size for a listening hole and a quick peek.

Dora used her hip to shove the washstand over and peeked through. The room next door was dark, but the pale moonlight filtering through the lacy curtain showed a simple wooden table surrounded by four chairs.

"Can I pop next door for a minute?"

The maid held out the ring of keys, with the key marked one sticking out. "Be quick. My pa will come looking soon."

Dora moved as fast as she dared, taking care not to make so much noise as to be heard below. Raucous laughter filtered up the stairs, providing her with plenty of cover. Someone was having a fun evening. Pity it wasn't her.

The lock tumbled with ease. Dora turned the handle and hit the lights. She paced across the room, estimating where the hole would be on this side. It was camouflaged so well that it took her a moment to find. A cheap framed print hung on the wall at the right height. The hole was aligned with a swirl in the metal frame. It looked like a shadow until you got right up to it.

"Utterly brill, Freddie," she whispered. Or maybe not, given Freddie was dead. Despite his impeccable work on the set-up, he must have been discovered. She wished she knew what mistake he'd made.

What was she going to tell Rex? He'd surely ask what she found. She couldn't lie completely, in case he came back again on his own. It would have to be the truth, or a variation on it, anyway.

The maid waited in the hall. She took the keys back after Dora locked the door and pocketed them.

"Are you sure you don't know the identity of the other man?" Dora asked. "Such information would be worth a *substantial* amount."

"I'll say," the woman muttered, shaking her head. "I'm guessing that's the kind of information that got your friend killed. I'm right glad I don't know. Don't bother asking my pa. He keeps a tight fist on his purse and even tighter control of his lips."

Dora nodded her understanding and fell into step beside the woman. She chattered away, carrying on about the room, as they descended into the main pub area.

"My Tommy'll be right pleased with the room. I'll get him, and then we'll go up." Dora turned to look at the table under the stairs.

It was empty.

The bottom fell out of Dora's stomach.

She hadn't been more than five minutes, ten at the max. All Rex had to do was sit there and drink.

A frustrated groan followed by a loud cheer in a familiar voice caught her attention. She tensed up and slowly pivoted in the other direction.

Rex's back was to her, but she'd know that blond hair anywhere. Was he pumping his fists in the air? And why was the sunburnt behemoth sitting across from him rising from his chair?

Dora's feet were in motion before her head caught up. She practically flew across the room in her rush to Rex's aid. The man was still sitting there, celebrating no less, while the rest of the crew around the table were scenting blood on the air.

Dora laid a hand on Rex's shoulder. He tipped his head back and graced her with a smile. "Darling! You're back, and just in time to witness my glorious victory. These dear men invited me to play cards with them. Lo and behold, I won every hand... which was convenient," he added, "since the funds were mine to begin with."

The behemoth wasn't nearly as thrilled with Rex's excellent showing. He shoved back his chair so hard that it tumbled over, striking the wooden floor with a clatter. He thrust a meaty finger in Rex's face. "You cheated us. I know it."

Rex reared back as though his face had been struck instead of his honour. "Now see here, Arnie, I did no such thing..."

Rex's opponent wasn't interested in Rex's assessment of his poker skills. The pub local looked his friends in the eye and wiggled his eyebrows in a silent call to arms.

"Aye, the toff cheated. I saw 'im pull a card from 'is sleeve," chimed in another man.

Dora didn't need to go back in time and witness the event to figure out what had happened. Rex had somehow given away his status. The locals pegged him as an easy mark and invited Rex to play cards.

Rex might be naïve, but he wasn't stupid. He'd doubtless perfected the art of bluffing and counting cards during the endless hands he played with his fellow members of the upper crust. The poor local souls didn't stand a chance of beating Rex at what was practically his own game.

In his shoes, Dora would have thrown the game, losing just enough to ensure she escaped with her life intact.

Rex, however, obviously hadn't foreseen this turn of the tables.

Dora had to do something to diffuse the situation. Arnie was already flexing his fingers into a fist.

She played the only card she had by plopping in Rex's lap. She threw her arms around his neck and hugged him tight, positioning herself to protect Rex from a blow.

"What a clever gent you are," she purred in her thick East London accent. She planted a smacking kiss on his smooth cheek and then whispered in his ear, "Follow my lead."

Dora loosened her hold and twisted to face the crowd of men gathering on the other side of the table. "No need for sour grapes tonight, boys. My dapper gent is here for the entertainment, not the funds. I'm sure he'll give you a chance to win your money back. Maybe with a new game?" She turned back to Rex and asked, "How are you with darts, sugar bunny?"

Rex's brow wrinkled as he searched Dora's face for some clue of the right answer. She gave a microscopic shake of her head. "Fair to middling, at best?" he said.

"The bloke's lying again," Arnie protested. "I'll not be taken for a fool. Let your girl play in your place and we'll see how well you get on this time around."

"I, err..." Rex stuttered, glancing again at Dora. This time, she gave a single nod of approval. "Well, why not? I've had my fun."

Dora feigned concern as she climbed to her feet. "I dunno... I've never played before. I don't know what to do."

Arnie wrapped an arm around her shoulders and pulled her against his sweaty side. "You can watch me and the boys. We'll show you 'ow it's done."

"That's mighty nice of you," Dora purred, batting her lashes. "I'll stand over there so I can keep a good eye on you."

Arnie and his friends were practically rubbing their hands together in glee while Dora sidled over to Rex.

She leaned against him, praying he'd paid attention during his French lessons at Eton. She couldn't risk any of the locals overhearing her instructions. In a low voice, she said, "Quand je lance la fléchette, cours. Tout suite!"

Rex's eyes flicked from her face, to the dartboard, and back to the main entrance.

Good. He'd understood. Dora leaned more of her body against his, subtly directing him to distance himself from the table. They managed to position themselves in line with a clear path to the door, one minuscule movement at a time.

Arnie and his friends took turns lining up and making their throws. The darts struck each time, earning the men higher and higher scores. Finally, it was Dora's turn. She sashayed past the men, winking at a few on her way to claim the darts. By the time she lined up to throw, every eye in the place was on her. Exactly as she'd intended.

She threw the first dart. It hit the wall, a hand's width to the side of the board's edge. The men snickered. She tittered and feigned embarrassment before shifting her stance and trying again.

The second throw went better. She hit the board, landing

just inside the second ring from the edge. Dora clapped in delight. "Did I win?"

The men laughed. Arnie patted her on the back. "Not yet. Throw the last dart and we'll see who takes home the bank, love."

Dora walked closer to the board and studied it. "Am I supposed to hit the outside circle or this little one in the middle?"

"The little one, not that it matters," Arnie added.

Dora paced away from the board, this time coming to a stop farther away than before. If anyone had cared to look, they'd have noticed she was standing right next to the table, piled with coins and pound notes.

Dora flipped the dart in her hand and licked the sharp point. "For luck," she explained, and then shimmied her hips. While every red-blooded man in the bar was distracted by her motions, she let the last dart fly. It flew dead straight with nary a wobble and landed in the exact centre of the board.

You could have heard a pin drop in the stunned silence.

Dora made her move. She lifted the edge of the table and shoved with all her might, sending the money falling to the ground. She was hot on Rex's heels when she raced out the door.

The pair didn't stop running until they were safely inside Liverpool Station. Dora had a stitch in her side and her brow was beaded with sweat, but that did little to cool her exhilaration. It wasn't until her pulse slowed and she caught her breath that she realised Rex was staring at her, dumbfounded.

"Who are you?" he blurted.

"I'm Theodora Laurent," she replied without missing a beat. "And don't you forget it!"

Chapter 11
Rex pays a call

B y mutual agreement, Rex and Dora remained mum on the
topic of their evening adventures until they reached the safe
confines of Rex's house in Mayfair. Rex poured them each a
Scotch and was much relieved to see his hand had stopped shaking.

After offering Dora a glass, he ignored her invitation to sit
beside her and settled into an armchair instead. The adrenaline
that had fuelled their escape was gone, leaving behind a curious
lightheadedness and an ache in his legs. Rex sipped the whiskey,
letting the burning warmth restore him to sanity.

Unlike him, Dora was calm and collected, with only a faint
blush on her cheeks left from their escapade. A hundred
questions flitted through his mind. Where was she born? How
had she risen from the gutter to her current station? When did
she master the art of throwing darts?

He pushed them all aside. There'd be time aplenty to delve
into her history once they were out of danger. Only one
question mattered right now.

"What did you learn from the barmaid?"

Dora made him wait until she took another sip of her drink

before responding. "Are you sure you want to know? I'm rarely shocked, but even I was confounded by what I learned." She grimaced and took another drink, as though she was warding herself against the memory.

Rex's mind raced faster than a thoroughbred out of the gate, flying past theories, each more outlandish than the last. His inner voice shrieked for him to turn back, but his conscience refused to heed the call. He'd never find justice for Freddie's death if he turned a blind eye to the distasteful.

"Tell me."

"Very well. The barmaid showed me to a room upstairs that had a rather unusual feature. A peep hole. Freddie paid her to sneak him upstairs so he could spy on the activities of a certain man."

"Activities?"

"*Activities*."

Rex blanched. Egads. The inflection in Dora's voice was enough to convince him to avoid further details. "I'm surprised the woman revealed that."

"The information didn't come cheaply, I assure you. She said Freddie was dead, and money was money. I did warn you of the risks associated with places such as that. You saw firsthand how quickly opinions of the hoity-toity can shift."

Rex rubbed the back of his neck, feeling ashamed of his reckless haste to venture into the seedier part of town. "Thank you for saving me."

"You're welcome. I trust you'll agree that we should draw a line under that avenue of investigation. If anything, we're lucky the detectives made such a hash of things. Imagine if they'd discovered the reason for Freddie's visits! He'd have made the front page, with his reputation reduced to tatters."

"To think, I presumed dying alone in a dirty alleyway was

the worst part of the matter," Rex muttered, half under his breath. "You've given me much to think about."

Dora gave him a sympathetic smile. "What will you do next?"

Rex gazed into his glass, hoping for inspiration. None of this had gone to plan. Had it been only this morning that he'd balled his newspaper and tossed it into the porridge? That couldn't be right. He'd lived several lifetimes alone during their sprint across Spitalfields.

Where had it all gone wrong? He'd been so clear-headed when he'd gone upstairs after breakfast. He'd asked Brantley about Freddie's household and ended up on Theodora's doorstep instead.

Perhaps it was time for Rex to stop taking suggestions from everyone else and go back to his initial intention. He mustered up his courage and said, "I'm going to pay a visit to Freddie's house and see if I can have a word with his valet. He likely has some idea of Freddie's movements on the days prior to his death."

"What if you don't like what you find?"

"We've dodged a bullet, raced across London by car and on foot, and I've discovered my best friend was a peeping Tom. I'm hard-pressed to envision how things can go any further downhill."

Dora leaned forward and rapped on the oak table, causing Rex to raise his eyebrows.

"What was that for?"

"I'm warding off the bad luck," she answered. "A statement like the one you made is far too tempting to the universe. If I had a shaker of salt, I'd toss a sprinkle over my shoulder."

Rex chuckled at the worry wrinkling Dora's brow. "I'll ask the maid to send some to your room. On that note, I'm going to turn in. Did you want to accompany me tomorrow?"

Dora brushed the invitation aside. "I rarely rise before noon, and especially not when I'm staying somewhere for a sleepover. I'll send one of the staff to find you when I'm fed, watered, and dressed. You can tell me what you learned then."

Rex felt a rush of relief at her reply. He hadn't a clue what excuse he'd have used to explain why he was escorting Theodora around town. He wished her goodnight and headed upstairs to turn in.

A restless night of sleep did little to quell Rex's nerves. He rose earlier than normal and called for a tray to be brought to his room. He wasn't up for questions from his grandmother. By ten, he was on his way out the door.

Recalling the challenges of the day before, Rex eschewed his stable of vehicles and asked one of the lads to hail him a taxi. It took but a moment to flag one down one of the ubiquitous black cars. Rex climbed into the back and rattled off the address.

"Right away, guv," the driver replied, filling the air with the smell of onions and garlic.

Rex lowered his window a crack and stared at the world outside, determined to avoid further conversation. The short drive barely gave him time to prepare a few words of explanation.

The curtains were drawn, and the knocker was missing from the front door. The implication was clear. Freddie's household was not receiving visitors. Rex didn't let the cold welcome stop him. He wasn't there to pay a call on the family. He asked the driver to drive on, directing him to the alley that ran between the towering houses lining the street. Rex stepped out at the kerb and did his best to avoid the mud and worse dotted along the pavement.

Soon enough, he spotted a gate with Freddie's house number. It opened with a loud scrape, sending a flock of birds flying into the air. The garden had an air of abandonment. The shed doors were closed tight, and the grass was overgrown. Would Rex find anyone at home?

He rapped lightly on the kitchen door. When no one answered, he inched sideways and peered through the window. A dirty bowl and cup sat beside the basin. Someone was staying there. Rex curled his hand into a fist and banged.

A stout, middle-aged man, fastidiously dressed in an old-fashioned dark suit, answered a few minutes later. Rex recognised him as Freddie's butler.

"Lord Reginald! I certainly didn't expect to find you back here. Apologies for the delay." The butler hurried him through the kitchen and up the stairs to the main floor. "I would offer you a cup of tea, but I'm the only one here. What can I do for you?"

"I'm terribly sorry to disturb you," Rex said by way of beginning. "I hoped to have a word with Freddie's valet."

"Were you thinking of hiring him? If so, I should tell you he's already found another position. The family let everyone go. I'm only here long enough to close up the house."

"Ahh," Rex sighed. He should have foreseen this outcome, knowing what he did of Freddie's finances. With Rex's help, Freddie had started earning a small income off some investments. He'd channelled most of it into keeping up appearances, remaining optimistic that he'd eventually attract a wealthy wife.

That family dream was as dead as the man who'd borne the title.

"Mayhap I could be of assistance? Did his lordship have something of yours here he failed to return?"

"Not exactly." Rex gnawed at the inside of his cheek. How to phrase the question? Should he ask for Freddie's diary? He wasn't entirely sure the man kept one. What if the butler demanded to know why... or worse yet, said no?

Needs must. Rex swallowed his pride and made his request. "I'm disappointed with the outcome of the police investigation. While they seem content to shelve the matter, I refuse to follow suit. I wondered if you might have a copy of Freddie's diary, or a list of his movements prior to his death. Anything you can tell me will be held in the strictest of confidence. You have my word."

The butler glanced from side to side, caught in an awkward predicament. The unwritten rules of butlering required absolute discretion. However, he was also expected to do anything he could to protect the family's reputation.

The family reputation won out, just as Rex had hoped.

"I don't have Lord Frederick's personal items. Those have been packed away. Nonetheless, I pride myself on meticulous record-keeping. I can offer you my notes of his lordship's movements in the last months. Where possible, I recorded which invitations he accepted and the nights he chose to dine at the club. Would that be of use?"

Rex could hardly believe his luck. Not only would that be useful, it was far more than he expected to gain. "That's marvellous, old chap! If it isn't too much of a bother, I'll copy down the information I need and promise to return them tomorrow."

The butler left Rex standing in the foyer while he disappeared to the lower floor to collect the item in question. Rex passed the time by looking around. He was disheartened by the blank patches on the walls where paintings had hung. He'd like to think they were in storage, but he was realistic enough to acknowledge the truth. In a month or so, they'd turn up on the auctioneer's block to raise much needed funds.

"Here you are, sir. I wrapped them in paper." The butler handed Rex a package the size of a small ledger. "Shall I call your car to come around?"

"I came by taxi," Rex explained. "I know it's unorthodox, but I'd prefer to exit the way I came in. No need to get tongues wagging before I've had time to make any progress."

"Of course, sir." The butler's frown belied his words, but he did as Rex asked.

When they got back to the kitchen, Rex noted with amusement that the dirty plate and cup were nowhere to be seen. The butler might not approve, but he'd foreseen the possibility of Rex's request and tidied up.

Rex got halfway out the door before another thought crossed his mind. "Pardon me, but I've been thinking about Freddie's family. His younger sister hasn't had her coming out yet, has she?"

The butler's eyebrows shot up to his hairline. "No, sir. She's still a year away, thank goodness. She can conduct her mourning in peace."

"If it isn't too much to ask, would you convey a message to her ladyship? When it comes time for her introduction to society, ask her to get in contact with my grandmother. I'm positive the Dowager Duchess would be pleased to sponsor her. It's the least we can do to honour Freddie's memory."

The butler broke character and beamed from ear-to-ear. "I'll do so at the earliest possible convenience. Take your time with the records, Lord Reginald. You are a truly excellent friend."

Rex spun around and left without saying another word, mostly to keep the butler from seeing the tears shining in his eyes. He dashed them away with the back of his hand while hustling through the garden. Good friend, indeed.

Until Freddie's death, he'd have sworn they kept no secrets of consequence from one another. Now, he was far from sure. Although he was loath to admit it, part of him was desperately afraid his golden view of Freddie would end up tarnished beyond recognition.

Chapter 12
Dora goes shopping

On the topmost floor of the dowager's Mayfair mansion, Inga stood in front of the dormer window with her arms crossed and a frown marring her normally implacable features. "This is beyond the pale, even for you, Dora. Give me ten minutes and I'll clear a path to the back gate."

"I don't have ten minutes. If I'm late, Victor will get antsy and leave," Dora replied, looking as cool as a cucumber. "Besides, I've made treks like this one multiple times in the past, and under worse weather. At least this time there's no snow."

Inga sniffed her disapproval, but slid over to clear the way to the window.

Dora swept in and pushed the bottom pane up. After checking no one was around outside, she hiked her skirt and stuck one foot over the ledge. At the last second, she reached over and patted her friend on the cheek. "Look on the bright side. If I fall to my death, you're my designated heir."

Inga rolled her eyes. "I'm sure your jewellery and clothing will bring me great solace during the difficult time. Don't die. That's an order."

Dora gave a salute and scampered onto the pitched roof of

the Mayfair home. The soles of her kid-skin slippers had been specially designed to provide extra grip in just these circumstances. She hurried up to the peak of the roof, hunching low to avoid detection from the street.

For the typical guest, Mayfair's Georgian and Edwardian homes had two entry points — the front door and through the garden at the rear. As a child, Dora's brother had introduced her to a third option. Scurrying across the roof wasn't for the faint of heart, but it was particularly useful when attempting to avoid the watchful gaze of a governess.

It was easy work to walk along the roofs, with nary a gap between the row of houses. So long, that is, if one was daring enough to try. It was with this plan in mind that Dora had crept out the night before and identified a hotel a few doors down.

Only a lone bird took note when she dropped onto the flat concrete roof. There was a line of chimneys, storage for rubbish, and a square hut with an unlocked door that opened to reveal a staircase. Taking care, Dora checked first to make sure the stairwell inside was empty before descending to the ground level.

Somehow she resisted the temptation to wave at the man working the front desk. It wouldn't do for him to remember her passing, especially if she needed to use this route again. By the time she emerged on the street out front, she was simply one more middle class woman on her way to do the weekly shop.

A careful application of make-up and a plain navy dress ensured no one gave her a second look. After a quick ride on the underground from Green Park, she emerged at Knightsbridge and headed above ground.

She moved automatically, winding between the people going back and forth on the streets. Now and then, she paused to buy something from a shop or stand. It wasn't that Dora needed anything in particular, especially not while she was a guest of the dowager. However, she knew from experience that the seemingly insignificant details were critical to pulling off a disguise. Housewives shopped, and therefore, so would she.

Part of her longed to extend her walk along Brompton Road until she reached the Victoria & Albert Museum. Her mother had taken the children to visit once. Dora and her brother Wills had sneaked off while their mother gazed at a cast recreation of some Greek artefact. Their mother had been livid when she found them half an hour later, standing in the garden fountain, wet from head to toe.

Dora could visit the museum any time she liked now that she lived in London. While she longed to revisit the displays, it was the ghosts hiding behind them that worried her. In every shadow, she feared catching sight of young Wills, up to mischief. Wills was long gone, one more victim of the Great War.

Dora wrenched her mind away, knowing that path led only to sorrow. She turned her thoughts instead to her upcoming meeting.

She hadn't been entirely honest with Rex when she'd declined to accompany him to Freddie's house. She hadn't needed to go along with him because she had already made arrangements of her own.

Rex would doubtless return home shortly, dismayed to have learned that Freddie's valet had flown the coop. That was because someone else had been paying the valet's stipend. Lord Audley insisted Freddie employ a member of his team, and the post of valet had been the only one vacant. Audley's man Victor had stepped in.

With Freddie dead and Dora assigned the case, Victor had no need to stick around. Still, he was wary of ending up like Freddie. He'd agreed to an early morning assignation so long as they met in a public place and kept it short.

Right on time, Dora strode through the doorway of Fletchers department store. Despite being mid-week, the store boasted plenty of foot traffic. Sales clerks stood behind counters showing their wares. Dora avoided their entreaties to view the latest styles of hats and gloves, her focus on the signs for the cafe.

The place was busy enough that she had to pause for a moment and scan the occupants to find the person she was due to meet. There was a table of four older women near the front window. The rich fabric of their dresses and handbags proclaimed their status as wives of the merchant class.

Behind them sat a young mum reading a magazine while a babe slept in her arm. Another table had been claimed by a pair of old men playing a game of chess. Had Victor stood her up?

He was there, but was so well hidden that she almost missed him. Victor sat at a corner table tucked behind a display case full of pastries. If Dora hadn't met him before, she'd have struggled to identify him. He was half hidden behind an open newspaper, with his face turned down to disguise his profile.

"You're late," Victor said, glaring at her from above his newspaper.

Dora ignored his grumblings, instead waving down a passing waitress so she could order a cup of tea and a teacake. When the waitress was out of earshot, she finally replied. "I had to wait until the servants were occupied with their duties. You know as well as I do how many bodies are in constant motion in the great houses. Please, tell me you brought it."

Victor closed his newspaper, revealing a pockmarked face above a brown wool suit. His black hair was slicked into place with oil. He folded the paper over a couple of times before handing it across the table. "You can take it. I finished it."

"Thanks, love," Dora replied. When she picked it up, she wasn't surprised to find it had an extra heft to it. He'd tucked a book within the society pages, of all places. The irony was not lost on Dora.

The waitress returned with Dora's order, setting the cup and plate on the now empty table. Dora slid the paper-wrapped book into her oversized shopping bag. Tucked in between a loaf of bread and a bag of apples, it was as safe as it could be from pickpockets.

After the waitress left them alone, Dora returned to their conversation. "I won't open it here. Can you give me a summary of what I'll find?"

"For the most part, there's little of excitement. The comings and goings of an upper-class gent become rather repetitive after a few weeks. The biggest excitement was when he tried some new cologne and I had to advise him against it. Once you arrived in town, he was hardly at home. Audley kept me stationed there for two months, and I've got nothing to show for it other than a recipe for boot polish. Although this is far from the ending I'd wished to see, I won't miss being assigned valet duties."

"What of the critical night?" Dora asked, keeping her voice low.

Victor shrugged. "Last I saw of him, he said he was off to check on you."

Drat. No help there. "What of the night before? Or that whole week, for that matter?"

Victor's mouth curled into a grin. "For the most part that week, he dined out at the club and turned in at a reasonable time. But when you get to the night before, you hit upon the interesting bit. His choice of wardrobe sent my eyebrows raising. When I asked for details, he admitted he was meeting with someone outside his social sphere."

Dora could hardly believe her ears. This was far better than she'd hoped. "Who was it?"

"A sailor!"

A sailor? Dora hated to admit it, but this information had her flummoxed. What would a young lordling have to do with a sailor? How and where would their paths have crossed?

Victor wasn't done. "Fred was like a dog with a bone during his last days in London. I caught him staring off into space more than once, lost in a world of his own. He asked me questions about how I got my start, and what other kinds of things I'd done."

"He did the same with me," Dora admitted.

"I assumed he was interested in taking a more active role in our organisation. Seemed harmless enough until he failed to turn up."

"That's always the case." Dora crumbled off a piece of her teacake and put it in her mouth. Despite the soft texture and rich layer of butter, it tasted of ash and regret. She drank her tea to clear the flavour from her mouth. "Think hard," she beseeched Victor. "Did he say anything else?"

Victor's eyes widened, and his voice rose until it was bright with indignation. "Do you think I haven't wracked my mind during the past week?"

Dora felt the eyes of the other occupants of the cafe burn into the back of her head. They were causing a scene. She pitched her voice loud enough to be easily overheard. "Don't worry, dear! I'm sure we'll find your mother's ring. It must be somewhere in the house." She reached over and took Victor's hand in hers, patting it gently. Slowly, the surrounding conversations resumed to their prior levels.

Victor leaned forward, narrowing the space between their heads. In a subdued tone, he said, "Fred refused to give me a name. I searched his diary and found a reference. Fred made note of a tattoo—a distinct one of a rising sun over blue waters. I've got a couple of friends on the lookout for anyone matching the description down by the docks. As soon as I get wind of who he is, I'll arrange to have a conversation."

"Make sure to book a table for three," Dora added. "The trail is cold enough as it is. If there's aught to be learned, I don't want to waste time filtering it through our layers of protection."

"But you're staying with—"

"Leave that part to me. I've got things well in hand, and I got away today without raising any eyebrows. Send word to Harris and I'll be there."

"Fine." Victor grabbed his hat and coat and made a production of getting ready to leave. In a normal voice, he bid her goodbye. "I'd better get back to the office. See you at home?"

"Of course. I'll settle the bill on my way out."

Victor departed the cafe without a backward glance, off to parts unknown. Dora hated leaving her only lead in his hands, but what else could she do? She'd have to be patient. Who knew? Maybe Rex would come up with something from his visit. Crazier things had happened.

She finished her tea and then made her own escape. On her way back through the department store, a hat display caught her eye. She detoured from her path and made quick work of purchasing the item that had got her attention.

She left the store with a hatbox in hand. Inside it, swathed in tissue paper, laid a white straw hat decorated with a yellow ribbon and an ostentatious clutch of French sunflowers. She couldn't wait to see the expression on Inga's face when she presented her gift and offered her explanation.

"Sunflowers to match your sunny disposition, darling. Isn't it the bee's knees?"

With any luck, the long walk and ride on the underground would prove long enough for her to master saying it without breaking into hysterics.

Chapter 13
Rex searches for clues

Rex was deep in thought by the time he returned home, once again using the rear entrance. So accustomed was he to being waited upon, he nearly walked face first into the terrace door. Fortunately, one of the housemaids was busy dusting and happened to spot him approaching. She rushed over and opened the door just in time to help Rex avoid a catastrophe.

Rex thanked the young woman while handing her his hat and coat. Before she could scurry off to hang them somewhere appropriate, Rex asked her to let Sheffield know he had returned.

The butler appeared in the library's doorway soon after, with his hands pressed against his side as he awaited his orders. "Welcome back, sir. I trust you had a pleasant outing. Would you like me to send for tea?"

"Yes, that would be lovely. Walking about town has left me parched. But before you go, do you know whether Miss Laurent is up and about yet?"

"She is awake, your lordship. Her companion rang for a

breakfast tray a half hour ago. As to whether she is dressed for the company, I couldn't say. Would you like me to inquire?"

"If it isn't too much trouble. Let her know I'll await her here in the library. She may join me at her leisure. There is no need for her to rush."

The butler gave a sharp nod of confirmation and departed, pulling the door closed behind him. Rex was left alone in the library with only the books to keep him company. Although the Rockingham collection of titles was vast and varied, Rex was more interested in the volume he had brought back home with him.

He eschewed the sofa where he had sat with Theodora the night before and instead chose a comfortable armchair near the rear window. The sunshine trickling in provided light enough for him to see the book.

Once he was settled, Rex opened the leather-bound tome and set to work deciphering the spidery handwriting that filled the pages. It took him some time to get the hang of how Freddie's butler had shaped his letters. Was that an *m* or a double *n*? Rex tilted the book to change the angle of the light and realised it was actually an *e*.

He barely looked up when the footman appeared with a tray bearing a pot of fresh tea and a cup and saucer. He did, however, take care not to spill a single drop on the handwritten pages.

Once Rex got the hang of the handwriting, he was engrossed in the contents. Most of the notes were dedicated to items such as money spent on household expenses, recipes for shoe and silver polish, and lists of wine and spirits to order. In between those mundane matters, Rex discovered what the world of the upper class looked like to a fly on the wall.

Freddie's butler had kept notes on every visitor. By his own name, Rex found a listing of his favourite food and drink, preferred topics of conversation, his distaste for cigars, and where he liked to sit when paying a call. Rex hadn't even been aware he had a preferred chair in Freddie's drawing room until he saw it written in black ink.

A glance at the wall clock showed more than an hour had passed. Rex's tea was long cold, but his interest in the book was fast warming. However, as much as he wanted to snoop on other members of his set, he knew Theodora would arrive at any moment.

The depth and breadth of information made Rex optimistic he'd find something of value. He flipped through the pages, keeping an eye on the dates at the top of each entry, until he got to the start of April. What had Freddie done in the weeks before his death?

By the time Dora sailed into the library, trailing silk scarves and floral perfume, Rex had an inkling of where to go next with their investigation.

"Good morning, darling," Dora drawled, once again using her French-touched accent. "Or is it good afternoon? When lounging at home, the hours simply run together."

"It's 2 PM," Rex answered, after glancing at the clock face. His stomach growled, reminding him he'd been up for ages. "Would you mind ringing the bell? I'm famished."

Dora pulled the thick tassel hanging on the wall. A footman responded and departed just as quickly, with a request for a plate of sandwiches from the kitchen. That matter resolved, Dora turned her attention to her new partner in crime.

"What's that you're reading, Rex?" she asked. She didn't wait for an answer, instead striding across the room to perch on the arm of Rex's chair.

Rex had to lean awkwardly in order to look her in the face, and even then, she was entirely too close. Until she'd arrived, the armchair had seemed spacious. Now, it was as though it had become a straightjacket, tying his body and his tongue into knots.

His defensive mechanism kicked in. If he wanted to keep a clear head, he needed to sit far away from Theodora. *From Miss Laurent*, he silently corrected himself. "Have a look for yourself," he blurted. He handed her the book and escaped from the chair. Now on his feet, he paced across the length of the room.

Dora arched her eyebrows, but if she had thoughts on his change in position, she kept them to herself. "From Freddie's butler?" she asked after perusing the first couple of pages.

"How did you figure that out so quickly?"

"When you've received as many handwritten notes from men as I have, even the worst penmanship proves little challenge. Besides, he wrote the name of the household right on the first page." She lifted the book and showed Rex the page in question. She resumed her skimming, commenting as she went along. "A case of Champagne Ayala! Freddie, you naughty boy! Keeping such a treat from me."

"The earliest entries are from the start of the year. Before your arrival," Rex added, unnecessarily.

"Indeed. I can't imagine such a fine vintage lasted too long in Freddie's home. I'll forgive him. On to more important matters. Is there a reason we're reading the butler's private papers and not Freddie's diary?"

"That journal was the best I could do. Freddie's staff had scattered on the winds, and his personal items were already in storage. The butler offered his notes on Freddie's movements. Better than nothing, I thought, so I took him up on it."

"An obedient servant is meant to be neither seen nor heard, but that hardly renders them blind and dumb. How often do we forget about the eyes and ears following our every move? And on that note..." Dora flicked her wrist in the door's direction. A second later, the knob turned, revealing the footman carrying a heavy silver tray. "Put it on the desk and we'll help ourselves to a light repast, won't we, Lord Rex?"

Rex nodded, although his head was spinning so much he hardly knew to what he was agreeing. How on earth had Theodora heard the footman's approach through the closed library door?

Dora set the book aside and rose to peruse the offering. "Cucumber with mint cream cheese! How did Cook know that was one of my favourites?" She offered Rex a china plate and then went to work helping herself to one of each type of finger-sandwich available. "I've done little more than lie abed today, and yet that hasn't dented my appetite."

The mental image of Miss Laurent lounging against his pillows, wearing only a satin peignoir, nearly made Rex's eyes cross. He swallowed, choked on air, and had to cough to clear his throat.

"Everything all right, Rex?" Dora asked with an air of innocence.

Rex blurted the first excuse that came to mind. "A bug flew into my mouth."

"Oh dear..." Dora punctuated her comment with a slant-eyed glance that made it clear she wasn't fooled.

Rex had to head the situation off before he made a fool of himself. An even bigger fool, that was. "Why don't we sit at the table," he suggested, pointing at the wooden table with reading lamps running along the middle. He would take one side, Theodora the other...

Dora swanned over and dragged a chair around so she could sit at the head. "This will make it easier for us to look at the book at the same time," she explained as she wiggled the other chair closer.

Rex shoved a finger-sandwich into his mouth to keep from

saying something he'd regret. With his back to her, he chewed furiously and warned his libido about dire repercussions should it continue to misbehave. He took a deep breath, filling his nostrils with her perfume.

"Silly me, I forgot to take a cup of tea!" she said, her shoulder brushing against his arm as she reached for the teapot.

Rex followed her to the table, only then realising she was wearing trousers. The wide-legged fabric stretched tight with every step, giving a tantalising hint of her slender legs. His willpower raised the white flag. He had no hope.

Of course, that was when Dora changed tack. She sat up straight, crossed her legs, and smoothed her face of all expression. "What did you learn? Was there anything in the journal we can use in our search for the culprit?"

Rex held back a sigh of relief and got down to business. "There were some anomalies in Freddie's behaviour during his final week of life. Several nights that week, his butler noted Freddie as dining out at a club."

Dora wrinkled her nose. "Isn't that what you men do for fun?"

"It wasn't the number of nights out that caught my attention, but the fact that they were divided between two different venues. I shouldn't admit this, but Freddie wasn't exactly overly flush with funds. As far as I know, he'd limited his subscription to Brook's, where his family had held a membership for generations. The butler noted another venue, however. White's, to be precise."

A hint of something flashed across Dora's face, but it came and went so quickly Rex didn't have time to identify the expression.

"Maybe he visited as someone's guest? Or he was testing out another option?" Dora offered. "I never have understood why you men want to spend so much time in those places, anyway. Without women, how fun can they be?"

"Err, yes, well," Rex stuttered. "Most clubs revolve around shared interests, be it politics, sports, or other activities. But White's? I can't think of a single reason for Freddie to darken their doorstep. They're notoriously conservative in their viewpoint, and very much home to the old guard."

"That does not sound like my Freddie," Dora agreed. "Was there anything else mentioned in the notes? Any visitors who were out of the ordinary?"

"For the most part, they were all members of our set. Freddie didn't entertain much at home."

Dora helped herself to another sandwich from her plate. She chewed daintily, flicking her tongue out to clean a spot of cream cheese from the corner of her lips.

Rex nearly groaned in frustration. He needed air. Distance. Space. Anything but to continue sitting here.

"What do we do next?" Dora asked. "Pay a visit to this club you mentioned?"

"Men only, I'm afraid. And, I'm not a member, either." Rex pushed back his chair and rose to his feet. "I find myself in need of some fresh air. A brisk walk often helps clear the cobwebs from my thoughts. I'll leave you here to finish your lunch. We can catch up again at dinner."

There was no other way to describe Rex's departure other than to say he scarpered as fast as his legs would move. He wasn't taking any risks that a certain female would ask to accompany him on his outing.

Rex knew exactly what type of woman Theodora was. Even if she hadn't been recently entangled with a friend, he had no intention of becoming her next prey.

Unfortunately, the gap between knowing and doing was

proving to be wider than he'd imagined. With his hat on his head and coat on his arm, he made himself a promise.

Even the devil herself wasn't going to distract him from his aim. Solving the mystery of Freddie's death was more important than anything else.

Chapter 14
Dora asks for help

Dora shut the door to her assigned room and leaned against its hard surface. Her stomach rumblings had little to do with the scene before her. The room was perfectly pleasant, from the cabbage rose wallpaper to the four-poster bed, and the idyllic garden view from the window. If pressed on the matter, her only complaint would be that it was too feminine.

The room had two advantages. The first was a connecting door to the next bedroom. Inga could sneak back and forth, pretending to be Dora whenever needed. The second was the sitting area between the bed and fireplace. The pair of chairs gave them a place to plot without having to worry about being overheard.

Inga was seated in one of the chairs, looking as though she hadn't moved a muscle since Dora descended to see Rex. She hadn't even allowed herself a break to partake of the still-steaming pot of tea beside her. At the sound of the door closing, Inga glanced up from her book to see Dora rubbing her stomach with one hand, while the other held a record book.

"Upsetting news?"

"More of a case of overindulgence. I shouldn't have eaten that third cucumber and cream cheese sandwich."

Inga shook her head and tsked an admonishment. "Moderation, dear. I don't understand how you can wrap your mind around the most arcane political ideologies, and yet cannot grasp this simple rule."

"Oh, I understand it just fine. It's far more interesting to thumb my nose at it than to let it guide my decisions. But enough about my problems. While I pour us both a cup of tea, tell me how you've been getting on and why you aren't reading Freddie's diary."

Inga lifted the book from her lap and peeled back one side of the dust cover. Underneath, Dora recognised the book she'd retrieved from Victor.

"I had to think fast when the maid delivered the tea. I'll be lucky to have anything for you before midnight. Freddie's handwriting is the worst I've ever seen. If that weren't enough, he also employed some kind of code to disguise people's identities."

"Perhaps I can offer something useful." Dora sank into the other chair. She passed Inga the book she'd brought with her from downstairs. "Freddie wasn't the only one keeping notes of the household activities. His butler kept a record of Freddie's comings and goings, along with details on his visitors."

"That will be a tremendous help!" Inga flipped through the first few pages. "I may yet make it to supper. How long can I hold on to this?"

"As long as you need. I used my feminine wiles to discombobulate Rex to the point that he had to escape. I doubt he'll return before you're done. If he does, tell him I brought it to you to read."

Inga lowered the journal onto her lap, crossed her arms, and speared Dora with a sharp look. "And where will you be?"

"Officially, or unofficially?"

"I'm more than capable of dissembling on my own. Stick to the facts."

"I'm off to the place I'd have visited if Rex hadn't shown up on our doorstep."

"Audley?"

"Nothing gets past you, old girl. I'll make my own way. No need for you to get up. The upstairs will be empty at this hour."

Inga shifted in her chair until she could hold both books in her lap. "Before you leave, you might want to get the key from my jewellery case."

"Key?" Dora spun on her heels. "What do you mean, key? You want me to lock you in here before I go?"

"Don't be ridiculous" Inga replied. "Given your penchant for using unexpected entrance and exit points, I thought it might behoove us to make it easier for you to come and go from the hotel. While you were out, I sent a note to Harris. He stopped by the hotel and rented a room. He told the staff that his wife and son would be joining him, and brought along a few items you might find useful."

Dora didn't need to be told twice. She hurried over to take the key. On her way out of the room, she made a detour to bring herself closer to her friend's chair.

Inga had already resumed concentrating on the two handwritten books. Therefore, she was caught off guard when Dora threw her arms around her shoulders.

Dora gave Inga a squeeze. "I don't say this often enough, but I hope you know I couldn't do this without you. I may be the face of this organisation, but there's an argument to be made about you being the brains."

Inga gave her dear friend a fond look and patted her on the arm. "When you put it that way, you make it sound as though I live a life of hardship. That couldn't be farther from the truth. I had every chance to say no when you invited me along for this adventure. No matter how many scrapes we get in, nor the number of times we've packed and moved, I have no regrets. We're family in all the ways that count."

Dora dropped to her knees so she could better look her friend in the face. "Let's keep it that way. I have so few people in the world with whom I can be completely honest. I do hope you feel the same. Should you and Harris ever want to make things official, or go a step further and have a child, please rest assured you always have my full support."

"Harris and I are happy enough with the way things are. If that changes, you'll be the second to know."

"The second? Who will be the first?"

"We'd talk to each other, you minx!" Inga swatted Dora with the journal. "No matter how bad the situation, surely we would have the wherewithal to hash out any problems together before we brought you into them." Inga tilted her head and glared Dora into submission with one of her infamous narrow gazes. "Speaking of family, have you decided when to get in touch with them?"

Dora dropped her gaze to the floor. "Not yet. I thought it best to wait until all this is over. I wish I could foresee how they'll react. Finding justice for Freddie might be a point in my favour. I'll need all the help I can get if I want them to overlook all my other life choices."

"If they love you, they won't need to overlook them. They will embrace them, the same way both Harris and I do. Have faith, Dora. There's never been any doubt about their love for you."

"Ah yes, but in a society built on titles, arranged marriages, and inheritance lines, love counts for little."

"We'll see. Now, go on with you. You can hardly expect me to cover for you forever. While I can do a passable enough job of mimicking your voice, pretending to be you at the dinner table is beyond my abilities."

Dora took care to check that the coast was clear before retracing her route from earlier in the day. Soon enough she was in their rented accommodation, grimacing while Harris fixed her tie. Finally, he proclaimed the fall of the silk to be perfect.

"How do I look?" Dora asked, backing up a step.

"Like your brother." Harris winked at her and then sent her on her way.

Whistling a jaunty tune she'd picked up in a New York nightclub, Dora parked her Hispano-Suiza at the kerb and swaggered up the front steps of Lord Audley's home. His formal title was the Duke of Montagu. As a member of the Order of the Garter, his importance to the Royal family was undeniable. What few knew was that Lord Audley oversaw a secret network of very well-placed spies that existed outside any government body.

Technically, Lord Audley was Dora's mentor and guide. Dora, however, preferred to see it as a partnership of equals. Nothing delighted her more than catching him off guard. Today's disguise was designed to do just that. She glimpsed her reflection in the picture windows on either side of the door.

To all the world, she appeared to be an upper crust young man in his late teens or early twenties. The collar of her coat and hat on her head kept her hair from giving her away. Her suit was courtesy of New York's finest tailors, and her shoes shone with fresh polish.

Audley's butler opened the door and gave her a dour stare. "Can I help you, sir?"

"I'd like a word with Lord Audley, if he can spare the time. I'm not expected," Dora answered in a gruff voice, passing him an embossed visiting card. On a whim, she'd had them specially printed with her dead husband's name and title. She'd been holding onto it for the right moment.

She watched as the butler read the name. It would mean little to him, just one more titled individual seeking his lordship's time. But Audley... Dora couldn't wait to see his reaction when he heard a ghost was requesting a moment of time.

The butler's expression brightened as he read the title on the card. "Of course, my lord. Please, make yourself at home in the drawing room while I check his lordship's availability."

Dora barely had time to admire the Monet gracing the wall of Lord Audley's drawing room before the man himself appeared. He hurried through the door with worry wrinkling his forehead and came to a dead halt when his gaze landed on Dora.

"Thank heavens. When Walters announced my visitor was a man, I was certain someone had uncovered your real identity. Perhaps you could warn me in advance the next time you adopt a new name," he said, sounding somehow both pained and relieved.

"And miss out on this fun?" Dora replied in a decidedly masculine voice. "Good to know I fooled the butler. Harris said the disguise was convincing, but I had some doubts."

"Don't let your head get too big. My butler long ago learned to turn a blind eye on the strange goings on in the house, your visits being no exception. But enough small talk. Sit down and explain to me why you've taken up residence in the home of one of London's most notorious gossip mavens."

"The dowager has a reputation for knowing all and seeing all, but not for telling all," Dora reminded Lord Audley. With a deceptive ease, she sank into a leather chair and crossed one leg over the knee. "She's delighted to have such a breath of fresh air as Ms Theodora Laurent staying in her guest room, especially since there's no risk of her social faux pas being discovered."

"There is that. Hopefully fear of repercussions will be enough to make her hold her tongue," Audley conceded, taking the seat on the sofa facing Dora. "However, moving in with the doyenne of the Ton was not on my list of approaches you might take toward this investigation. Given you are doing me a favour, I'll withhold judgment on the situation until I've heard a full explanation. Please, I beg of you — start at the beginning and leave nothing out."

Dora launched into a concise recount of her movements over the previous few days. Audley's expression drew more and more grave as she went on. When she finished, he sat for a moment, staring off into space.

"Freddie's father must be rolling over in his grave. I promised the man I'd keep an eye on Freddie and this happens. I never should have pulled the young lord into my web. This is my fault."

"It's all our fault," Dora chided. "Victor and I wound Freddie up with tales of our exploits. We were all blind to what he was thinking. I came here to see if you might have additional information to share, especially since my neck is now on the line. Getting shot at is a very effective motivator."

Audley rubbed his chin and pondered her words. "Rex had made a nuisance of himself in the days following Freddie's death. He made plenty of visits to the Yard and wasn't quiet about his intention to see the case solved. It's distinctly possible that Freddie's killer wanted to scare him off, and you happened to be in the wrong place at the time."

Dora cast her mind back to the event in question. Rex had gone to the car first. She'd followed with her hat and wrap. "The gunman had plenty of time to aim for Rex before I came out to the car. Maybe he was waiting to see what Rex did, and my presence spurred him on… or perhaps the message was meant for me. Is that a risk you want to take?"

Lord Audley didn't hesitate. "No. Although you are technically on a sabbatical, England has invested a sizeable amount in building your cover story. I've no desire to toss aside those years of your life or the time spent making Theodora Laurent into flesh and blood. I concur with your decision to team up with Rex."

Dora's lips wrinkled. "Team up isn't the right description. Rex has no idea of the bigger picture, and I'm hardly sharing quid pro quo. I'll admit, getting the butler's journal was useful, but beyond that… I don't dare tell him anything at all for fear we'll end up with another Freddie on our hands."

Her statement had the desired effect. Audley dropped that avenue of conversation and moved onto more solid ground.

"You've made admirable progress in the last twenty-four hours. What are your next steps? Do you need something from me? I know I've dropped you into this, but I didn't have anyone else to whom I could turn."

Dora flushed under his praise. Lord Audley had grown into something of a father-figure for her. He was her main point of contact for sharing the information she uncovered. On more personal matters, he also provided an incredibly discreet channel for her to communicate with her family. They may not know who or where she was, but they had confirmation that she lived, and vice versa.

But now wasn't the time to think about her family. Freddie's death came first. What did she need from Audley?

"I've two questions to ask before I make my way out. First, did the Yard hand over any notes on their investigation?"

"No, and for an excellent reason. As soon as I got in touch, they switched from clue-gathering to box ticking, and little else.

I put the fear of the Crown into them if they mucked anything up."

Dora tipped her hat to him. "That segues nicely into my second question. Rex has identified some unusual activity on Freddie's part, mainly in visits to White's. Can you think of any reason Freddie went there? Was it something you asked him to do?"

Like Rex, Lord Audley was mystified. "White's is no more my scene than it was Freddie's. Sounds like a productive direction for you to explore. Keep me in the loop on anything you find."

Dora knew a dismissal when she heard one. She hopped to her feet and executed a perfect salute. "Orders received, your lordship."

Then she ruined it all by swinging her hips as she waltzed out the drawing-room door.

Chapter 15
Clark pays a visit

R ex came back from his walk with a renewed fortitude.
He'd seen many beautiful women. As a landed member
of high society, he could have his pick of film stars, debutantes,
and even the more experienced divorcees.

In short, his life would not crumble if he avoided a dalliance
with Theodora Laurent. Now, he only had to convince the
animalistic part of his brain that this was true.

Brantley was waiting in his room when he got upstairs.
"Your grandmother has dictated black tie for dinner. I've
brushed your suit and pulled a selection of cufflinks for your
perusal."

"Thank you, Brantley," Rex said to his valet. He'd much
prefer a quiet dinner en famille or even a tray in his room.
However, Rex knew better than to argue. He'd have more luck
sharing his opinion with the wind or the tree outside his
bedroom window. What grandmama wanted, grandmama got.

His grandmother would not include any outside guests, not
while Theodora was here. But apparently she wasn't letting go
of the trappings of society just yet.

"Brantley, have you any experience with women problems?"

Rex glanced up in time to see Brantley biting his lip to keep from laughing. He felt his cheeks grow warm, but it was too late now. He'd waded into the water of this discussion, so he might as well see it through to the end. "Go on, man. Let's hear it."

"Apologies, my lord. I don't mean to poke fun at you. I assume it's Miss Laurent who has you so tied up in knots. If anything, it's reassuring to know that she's got the attention of all of us, yourself included."

"I blame her perfume. When she is on the other side of the room, I can almost keep my wits about me. However, she has the most damnable habit of sidling up next to me, allowing her scent to fault my brain."

Brantley chuckled. "You can think what you like, your lordship. I can't say I've got close enough to her to know what she smells like. But if you will pardon my honesty, I'll admit that particular feeling hasn't stopped her from playing a starring role in my fantasies."

Rex had no idea how to respond to this confession. He decided to direct the conversation onto safer ground by asking his valet for his recommendation on which of the cufflinks to choose. Brantley no doubt recognised the rationale behind Rex's request and launched into a verbose debate of the pros and cons of the nearly identical accessories.

Nonetheless, Brantley's words continued to circle in Rex's mind while he submitted to a fresh shave and steam, and then dressed for dinner. By the time the footman served the first course, Rex had come to a new conclusion.

While it was true that he had fallen for her act, he could hardly be blamed. Theodora Laurent was an expert because she had to be. Unlike him, she had not been born with a silver spoon in her mouth and the wealth of the world at her fingertips.

Rex was not the type to begrudge any of the self-made men of London their accomplishments. He could hardly proclaim himself a modern man if he looked down upon Theodora. He would be much better off indulging in her presence now, while he was living under the restrictions of his grandmother's edicts, than later when Theodora returned to her own home.

If there was one thing Rex knew for sure, it was that his grandmother would never approve of him taking up with a woman like Theodora Laurent. Theodora's unique perspective on the world equally entranced both him and his grandmama. Her larger-than-life presence captivated them. However, his grandmother was no more likely to proclaim their friendship to the world than he was to propose a lasting relationship with Miss Laurent.

The tension bled from Rex's shoulders. He looked upon Theodora's breathtaking countenance with clear eyes.

The rubies on her throat and ears blazed in the candlelight of the dining room. Her gown dipped low enough to hint at her décolletage, but not so much as to raise his grandmother's eyebrows. Rex was half-desperate to pluck one of the red feathers adorning the straps of her dress and trace it along the luminescent skin of her bare shoulders.

There was no doubt about it. Theodora was glorious.

Over dinner, she regaled the group with tales of her recent adventures in Egypt, where she'd seen the Sultan take the title of King, snuck into the palace to have tea with his wife, and toured the archeological digs at Thebes on the arm of Howard Carter. The detailed retellings carried an air of authenticity that was impossible to fake.

At the end of that tale, his grandmother laid her hands on her chest and issued a deep sigh of longing. "Oh, to spend a week in your shoes, Miss Laurent. If I were a half decade younger, I'd demand you take me along wherever you go next."

"If you were a half decade younger, I'd be afraid you'd end

up leading me into trouble," Dora quipped back. "The world would certainly tremble at our friendship."

The dowager laughed at her wit. "Come now, let's deport ourselves to more comfortable surroundings, where we can enjoy a glass of Madeira and swap more memories. Unless there is something else you wish to discuss," she added, glancing at her grandson.

"We've hit a wall in our investigation. I'm sure there is a way around it, but for now, it escapes me. A quiet night in is just the thing we need to rest and regroup for whatever comes next."

"I agree," Dora said, adding her support. She stood and came around the table to link arms with the dowager. "Wait until you hear about the oasis I visited. We had to travel for two days by camelback to get there. When we arrived, I ran into the most handsome Bedouin—"

Left in their wake, Rex offered his arm to Inga. He wasn't disappointed. He'd hoped to have a word with her, and now was the perfect time. "Dora said you had another look through the butler's journal. I don't suppose you spotted any other anomalies?"

"Other than being overcharged by the vegetable man, no. And I can't see profiteering off the elite as a killing matter. Can you?"

"If only it were that simple. I appreciate you taking a closer look." Rex slowed his steps, allowing Dora and his grandmother to get out of earshot. "Tell me, Miss Kay, how long have you known Theodora?"

Inga gave him a strange smile. "I've known Miss Laurent for her entire existence. She offered me the chance to escape the life of a spinster and accompany her on her adventures instead. Now that you've spent a few days with her, can you blame me for my choice?"

"Blame? Not hardly. Envy would be more appropriate."

Inga's steps slowed even further until she came to a halt in the corridor. She twisted her lips, as though wrestling with some inner turmoil. Finally, she opened her mouth and said what was on her mind. "Are you familiar with the myth of Daedalus and Icarus?"

Rex raised his eyebrows. "The boy who flew too close to the sun? It's been a long while since I read it, but I believe I can remember the basics. Why?"

"Think of me as Daedalus for a moment. Theodora is far brighter and far more deadly than any sunshine you've ever known. Bask now, but be wary of flying too close for too long."

Rex's expression softened. "Fear not, Miss Kay. I'm well aware of what kind of woman Theodora is. As soon as the current matter is resolved, I have no doubts that our paths will move in opposite directions."

Inga tilted her head to the side and studied him. Rex felt as though he was undergoing an assessment, but he wasn't sure for what.

"You're a good man, Lord Rex. Never forget that." Inga didn't wait for him to comment before turning around and heading into the drawing room. She joined the dowager at the card table and Theodora waved for Rex to match wits over a game of chess.

Rex relished the opportunity to pit his intellect against Theodora, this time on his home turf. The game moved back and forth, each capturing pieces in their fight for domination over the board. He was at risk of being checked when he heard a commotion in the hallway.

"Don't bother telling me he isn't home," a man's voice insisted. "He's hidden himself away for long enough."

Rex bit back a groan. He knew that voice. Only one man would be daring enough to force his way into the home of the Dowager Duchess of Rockingham.

"Lord Clark!" his grandmother yelped when the man in question burst into the drawing room. Like Rex, he was dressed in black tie, although his tie hung loosely around his neck and his top button was undone. The man was tall and slender, with a lean, athletic build. His hair was thick and wavy, styled in a fashionable side part, and his sharp features were accentuated by a neatly trimmed moustache.

Clark skidded to a halt at the sight of the foursome. His mouth dropped open. He made two steps forward, swaying as though the tectonic plates of the world were shifting under his feet.

Sheffield, the butler, arrived a bare second later, waving his age-spotted hands in apology before he even made it through the door. "I'm so sorry, your grace He pushed past me…"

"It's all right," the dowager assured the butler. "He's here now, so you might as well take his coat and hat. Clark, do be a dear and close your mouth."

Clark did as she asked and rubbed his eyes. "Have I somehow stumbled into an alternate timeline? Surely that cannot be Theodora Laurent sitting in your drawing room." He flopped into a nearby chair and stared unabashedly at the young beauty.

"I can see convincing you to leave will be out of the question." Rex laid his king on its side, declaring the game at an end, and rose to his feet. "I'll pour you a drink and let you in on the secret."

It took a measure of Rex's finest whiskey before Clark fully grasped the seriousness of the matter at hand.

The dowager's mouth had flattened into a bloodless line. She gave Clark one of her imperious glares. "If you breathe a word of this to the outside world—"

"You'll bar me from society. Yes, I know," Clark intervened.

"Oh no," the dowager replied, her eyes practically shooting

flames, "being barred would be too good for you. I'll do something far worse, such as telling every mother of an eligible daughter that you are in the market for a wife."

Clark paled and swayed in his seat. "They'd eat me alive!"

"Exactly. Behave, and you have nothing to worry about, young man."

Clark gulped. Dora covered her mouth with her hand and loosed a giggle. Clark held out his glass in a silent request for a refill. When Rex ignored him, he helped himself to the bar cart. On his way back to his seat, he detoured past Dora's chair.

"I've been terribly remiss in not introducing myself. I'm Clark Kenworthy, better known in society as the eldest son of Earl Rivers. Now that I've met you in person, I understand why Freddie kept you tucked away. It would have been swords at dawn if the rest of us had known the honour of escorting you was on the table."

Dora brushed his compliments aside, all the while making sure to position herself so her best features were on display. "You naughty boy! I'm hardly a plaything for you lot to fight over. I do have a mind of my own."

"And quite a quick one," Rex added, giving Clark a dark look of warning.

"In that case, I'll have to convince you I'm the better choice as soon as your evenings are free. Come now, how far along did you get with your search for the true cause of Freddie's death? Surely our Rex can't be the only one of service."

"We're making steady progress on our own..." Rex began, but Dora cut him off.

"I don't suppose you are a member at White's?" she asked Clark, fluttering her lashes prettily.

Clark's eyes lit up at her opening words, but he was crestfallen by the end. "What I wouldn't give to say yes! But why White's? Any members of such an establishment will be far too conservative to appreciate your fair graces."

"You'd be amazed how many starched shirt men have come running at the crook of my finger, Lord Clark, but in this case, that's the furthest thing from my mind. I'm not looking to catch the eye of a member. I need their guest book."

Clark didn't bother asking why. He smoothed his fingers over his moustache with one hand, his elbow resting on the other. With a slight shift in position and a lot less clothing, he could have been mistaken for Rodin's The Thinker.

Rex sat back and awaited Clark's thoughts. Like Freddie, he'd known Clark since their school days. If Freddie was the great defender and Rex the loyal friend, Clark was the devious mind within their group. If anyone could see a way out of this conundrum, it would be him.

Rex wasn't surprised when Clark shot to his feet with an elated grin.

"I've got it!"

"Let's hear it," Rex said, bracing himself.

"We're going to steal it, right out from under their noses." Clark skimmed the room, wiggling his eyebrows in encouragement. At the perplexed expressions on everyone's faces, he gave a huff of annoyance.

"I hate to be a downer, but won't we get caught?" Dora asked, her tone gentle.

"Of course! That's half the fun. You'd understand better if Freddie had brought you out with us, even once. Since he didn't, I'll explain. Every few weeks, we round up our friends and set off in London, with no mission other than to cause mischief and mayhem. Begging your pardon, Lady Rockingham."

"I'm well aware of your foibles," Rex's grandmother replied. "In this rare instance, I might be swayed into giving approval."

"We'll keep it our secret," Clark replied, giving the dowager an exaggerated wink. "Rex and Theodora, get your coats. We'll make a night of it. Three stops before dawn, with White's in the middle. They'll write off our antics as fool's play and none will be the wiser."

Rex glanced at Theodora and was delighted to see the admiration shining on her face.

"Mild mannered crime is my second favourite pastime, Lord Clark."

"And your first?" Clark asked innocently while he offered Dora his arm.

Dora may have been answering Clark's question, but when she spoke, she was looking Rex in the eye. "The night is young and so are we. Play your cards right and maybe you'll get the chance to find out."

Chapter 16
A visit to White's

Dora had not lied when she'd told the men they needed the guest book. Despite having both Freddie's diary and the butler's household journal, Inga had no luck in identifying the reasons behind Freddie's visits to White's.

That the man had been up to something, they had no doubts. His diary was littered with references to meetings in secret locations with people known only by their codenames. Unfortunately, none of these meetings had taken place inside Freddie's home. Therefore, the butler's journal couldn't offer any insights or clues.

Throughout dinner, while regaling the family with tales of her adventures, Dora's subconscious was busy gnawing away at the challenge. When Rex's friend Clark had made his surprise appearance, Dora felt as though a ray of sunshine pierced the darkness clouding her mind.

Their shenanigans were the perfect cover for a theft. Although she had feigned ignorance, she was well aware of the asinine antics of Freddie's set. It was part of why Lord Audley had drafted Freddy into his service in the first place.

In the non-stop goings on of the previous two days, Dora

had forgotten about Freddie's penchant for mischief. Of course, as soon as the words left Clark's mouth, she knew it was the perfect solution.

"Help me with my coat and wrap, will you?" Dora asked, glancing at Clark over her shoulder. His interest in her had not escaped her notice. Although she had no intention of going beyond casual flirting, she was not above using every advantage available.

Rex was doing his best to seem unconcerned with his friend's interest in his houseguest. But Dora couldn't help but see he was keeping a very close eye on their interactions.

"Let's review the plan one more time," said Rex. "Clark, we are taking your car. You will tell everyone that you called on Theodora and invited her out. Then, the two of you came to collect me. You are not, under any circumstances, to say that she is staying here."

Clark nodded in confirmation. "Have no fear! Your grandmother's threat is more than enough to buy my silence. Besides, your motives are pure. Like you, I want to see Freddie's death avenged."

The trio settled comfortably into Clark's Rolls-Royce Phantom and sped off through the night. They made a few stops along the way to round up other members of their gang of friends. Dora was thrilled with the welcome receptions she received from both the men and the women.

For the first time in years, Dora found herself enjoying the company of her peers.

Her real peers.

Unbeknownst to all of them, she had a claim to titles and estates. Not that she'd let on to that fact, however. The truth of her identity was a secret she would only tell to those she trusted with her life. For now, that list was short. Inga, Harris, and Lord Audley knew the name with which she had been christened at birth. To everyone else, she was forever Theodora.

After collecting the last member of their party, the group's first stop was an offbeat pub in an unfashionable part of town. The pub was a bustling, lively space, with a throng of working-class patrons gathered around the bar. The air was thick with the smell of alcohol and sweat, and the noise level was high, with the sounds of laughter, shouting, and clinking glasses mingling together.

There, the proprietor was happy enough to pour them each a pint in exchange for a very generous tip. He ushered them into a back room and closed the door, leaving them to make merry without rubbing elbows with his regular patrons.

Dressed as they were in their finery, they looked like a flock of peacocks parading through a stable. The pub's jumble of tables, scarred floors, and panelled walls made for a strange backdrop for the young popinjays.

Dora chose a seat next to a brunette. She was a waif of a woman, with wispy hair, pale skin, and huge, bug-like watery-blue eyes. Despite her muted appearance, her choice of clothing and braying laugh ensured she would never be missed. Tonight's attire comprised a vibrant orange floral blouse, navy wide-legged trousers, and a cowboy hat festooned with daisies. When Dora leaned close to have a word, she realised that the daisy petals were made of white and pink silk and their centres of dozens of tiny citrines.

"How does all this work?" Dora asked, waving a hand at the larger group.

"It's like a scavenger hunt. Clark sets the theme and an item to retrieve as we cross each location off our list. We hand everything over to Clark at the end of the night, and his butler ensures the items are returned unharmed. Or mostly unharmed. We learned the hard way that the ravens from the Tower don't like to ride in cars." The woman threw back her head and brayed like a horse, attracting everyone's attention. She caught her breath and explained, "I was telling Theodora about our misadventure in the Tower."

"A worst-case scenario," Clark assured her. "But at least you now have an idea of what to expect. Tonight's adventure will ideally be less *feather some*, but equally entertaining." He waited a moment, letting the interest in the room build. "After much soul-searching and thought-wrangling, I have come up with a suitable theme. In honour of our illustrious guest, the theme will be *'Behind Closed Doors'*. Should you choose to take the challenge, you'll join us in visiting three members-only societies — all of whom bar or discourage women from entering. For our first task, we will retrieve a fishing rod from The Flyfisher's Club in Piccadilly."

The waif squealed in delight. "My brother's a member. I do so love to tweak his nose."

"Then you must take the lead when we arrive," Clark replied. "Our second stop will be White's. Their biggest secret is the names of the illustrious men who venture inside. Therefore, it's their guest book that I desire. Our last stop will be none other than the House of Lords, where I expect you to retrieve a member's robe."

"The House of Lords?" Rex barked, staring at Clark as though he had three heads. "Have you gone mad? We'll never get inside at this hour!"

"We can and we will... because I have a key." Clark pulled a brass key from his pocket and brandished it for all to see. "Now, unless someone else has a concern to raise, I suggest we begin. The night is young, but we have many miles to travel before the dawn."

"And don't forget all the stuff-shirt men to anger," called another of the group.

With that, the group burst from the back room and out the front door, swamping the street with their gales of laughter and easy-flowing good humour. Dora piled into Clark's car, sitting in the back with Rex, while the waif took the front seat beside Clark.

As they drove off into the night, Dora felt the familiar thrill of adventure shoot up her spine, down her arms, and out to her fingertips. Her eyes were bright with enthusiasm, and her entire face glowed with happiness. Laughter bubbled freely from her lips when Clark raced past a bus, honking and waving at the passengers.

These moments were why she'd chosen to abandon her family and embrace the wilder side of living. Yes, one might argue that she could be here regardless, but none of the others knew even half the adventures she'd seen. Paris, Rome, Moscow, and even New York had played host to her, throwing open their doors to welcome her inside their inner circles.

Clark, Rex, and the young woman upfront would someday have to grow up and settle down. But not Dora.

The Flyfisher's Club proved little challenge. A couple of old men smoking cigars shouted in fury, but otherwise allowed the group to escape unharmed. High on the excitement, they headed straight for White's.

Located on St. James, barely a stone's throw from Rex's abode, the wrought-iron railings, Greek columns, and ornate balconies proclaimed luxury and wealth. Getting past the doorman would be the challenge.

By mutual agreement, the bulk of the group hid out of sight, ducking behind cars and shrubs. Rex and Clark stuck their noses in the air and marched up the front steps, looking to all the world like members.

From her hiding spot, Dora watched as Clark knocked on the door and began speaking with the club's doorman. He waved his hands in the air, emphasising some point. Before long, he was able to talk his way through the door. While Clark distracted the man inside, Rex held the door open and motioned for the rest of them to hurry.

Unfortunately for White's management, they'd chosen their doorman for his stately appearance and dignity, and not for his ability to slow a mob.

"I say! Well, I never! I say, there!" he shouted nonsensically, to overcome to string together a proper phrase. The man's grey eyebrows disappeared into his hairline and he cried in dismay when he realised the worst of the indignity. Not only was he overrun, but the mob included women.

Dora waved her fingers and blew him a kiss as she sauntered past. She soon picked up her pace, hurrying along a hallway in search of the manager's office. The others in her group fanned out, spilling into sitting rooms and dining areas. Their job was to provide a distraction while she nabbed the goods.

A chorus of furious shouts echoed in her wake.

Heavy footfalls caused her to turn around. It was Rex, rushing to catch up. "Down here," he said, pointing to a hallway. "I came here once or twice before the war. The office is this way."

The late hour worked in their favour. The office was empty, the lights off. Dora turned them on and scanned the room. She didn't have to look far. The gilt-edged guest book sat prominently in the middle of the desk.

Dora crossed the room as fast as she could and scooped their precious find from its place. "Got it! Let's go!"

She didn't have to tell Rex twice. They turned off the light and ran back into the hall, with Rex again in the lead. When they reached the main corridor, their escape plan hit a wrinkle. The way was completely blocked.

Unlike The Flyfisher's Club, White's had a fair few

members on hand to rush to the doorman's defence. A cluster of the more muscled members were busy strong-arming Rex's friends out the front door.

A distinguished older man wearing a military uniform spotted the pair. He was a striking figure, with a rugged, weathered look that spoke of a life spent outdoors. "Lord Reginald!" he shouted, burning them with his gaze. "Come back here!"

To give Rex his due, he didn't hesitate. "Sorry, Major!" he squawked. He spun around, grabbed Dora's arm and pulled her deeper into the building. In a low voice, he muttered, "There must be a back entrance."

Dora clutched the volume against her chest and moved as fast as her skirt and heels would allow. Feathers fell from her shoulders, leaving a line of ruby red across the royal blue carpet. She was too busy keeping pace to notice the trail of figurative breadcrumbs in her wake.

They turned again, following the hall, and finally spied the exterior door. Rex let go of Dora's arm and hurried ahead to get the handle.

Dora had almost caught up when she felt a thick arm wrap around her waist. "Rex!" she shouted. As soon as he looked back, she tossed him the guest book, heaving with all her might. It hit Rex in the chest and sent him staggering, but he wrapped his arms around it and pulled it close.

A man's voice growled over Dora's shoulder, shouting for Rex to stop. They were so close to getting the last piece. While the mystery man tightened his hold on Dora, she motioned for Rex to go. She was confident in her abilities to talk her way out of trouble, but less convinced they'd let them leave with the guest book in hand.

Right now, the guest book mattered more than anything else.

Rex came to the same conclusion. He mouthed an apology, opened the door, and leapt down the rear stairs.

The critical matter sorted, Dora gave up the fight to free herself. She twisted around to get a look at her captor. His hair was a deep, sun-bleached blond, brushed back in an easy, windswept style. He had a strong, square jawline and a cleft chin, but it was the dark shadows under his eyes that gave her pause. Dora lifted her gaze a fraction and found herself staring into a pair of emerald eyes.

It had been almost a decade since she'd seen them, if you excluded the fact that she saw the exact same shade every time she looked into the mirror.

Time passed and memories faded, but some things one never forgot. The shape of the face of a sibling was one of them.

Dora's eldest brother, for it could be no one else, was fuming. He was wild with anger, grabbing her arms in a bruising grip.

Dora was certain that he had no idea who she was. He was spitting mad at this unknown person who had dared to encroach upon his precious private territory. He'd seen a skirt and shapely legs, the trail of ruby feathers, and lost his wits.

Dora had a split-second decision to make. She could hold tight to her false identity and spend the next hours arguing for her freedom. Rex and Clark were high enough placed to eventually see her freed. But in the meantime, word would get out about what they'd done.

They couldn't afford that.

Therefore, Dora made the gut-wrenching decision to do what was best for the mission, her personal life be damned. She raised onto her toes, looked her brother in the eye, and uttered the magic words that would set her free.

"Benedict Cavendish! Let me go this instant, or else I'll tell Mama!"

Chapter 17
The short list

Rex had no intention of leaving Theodora behind. He dashed around the side of the building and spotted the rest of their group climbing back into the cars. Rex waved the book in the air to get Clark's attention. "We got it, but Theodora is still inside. Take the book and the others, and continue with the adventure. I'll get Theodora out, one way or another, and then see her home. We are close enough to walk."

Clark needed no further explanation. He trilled a piercing whistle to get everyone's attention and told them to move out. The group was far too busy hurrying to their cars to notice they were leaving two behind.

Rex didn't waste time worrying about what they'd think when they eventually noted Rex and Theodora's absence. It wasn't the first time they'd run into a snag during their adventures. Rex had proven himself to be adept at talking them out of trouble.

The only thing making Rex's guts clinch was concern for Theodora. Yes, she had told him to run, but would she know he'd come back? In her shoes, he would feel far from sanguine.

He spared a last second to debate how to handle his next

move. The front entrance was still crowded with people. Rex turned around and raced back the way he had come. In the shadowy darkness of the narrow lane, he nearly ran headfirst into Dora.

"You got out!"

"Of course I did," Dora replied, shrugging her shoulders as though it had been a foregone conclusion.

"But how? Who?" Rex was too flabbergasted to string together a complete sentence. He'd pictured himself arriving like a knight in shining armour to rescue a teary-eyed and very contrite Theodora. Instead, the damsel had rescued herself.

Dora pinched his cheeks and beamed at him. "Darling, I told you before we left. Oftentimes it is the uptight men in this world who are the first to loosen their collars. All it took was a promise to let the gentleman take me out for a drink, and he set me free. Between you and me, I'd have let him do it, anyway. But don't tell him that." Dora wiggled her eyebrows. "What happened to the others?"

"I sent them on without us."

"And the book?"

"I gave it to Clark for safekeeping. He'll bring it over first thing tomorrow. Or, I should say, first thing after he rises. I highly doubt it will be before noon."

"I've always said that the only good things that happen before noon are activities that carry over from the night before." Dora linked her arm through Rex's and turned him back toward the street. "Let's get home before anyone else spots us. My dress is moulting, my hair is muss and I think I may have actually broken a sweat. If someone were to see me right now, it would absolutely ruin my reputation."

Rex glanced at the woman on his arm as soon as they passed under a streetlamp. Despite her concerns, he still thought her to be one of the most glorious women in the city. Rather than undermining her beauty, the evening's exertions made her seem even more as if an exotic bird.

That night, Rex dreamt he was trapped in a golden cage. On the other side of the bars flew dozens of vibrantly coloured tropical birds. His calls for help were lost in the cacophony of squawks and caws. The birds flew round and round, but always remained a hair's breadth out of reach. When he awoke the next morning, Rex wasn't sure whether the dream had been a nightmare or foreshadowing of what was to come.

His grandmother was waiting for him at the breakfast table. She barely gave him time to take his first sip of coffee before pouncing on him with questions.

"Dare I ask whether you accomplished your task? I've already received a missive from Major Hobart demanding an explanation for your behaviour. The sheer cheek of that man! They may have pinned medals to his chest, but that hardly gives him the right to make demands of someone of my stature! Not that I owe the man any reply, but it would be reassuring to know that any trouble you caused was justified by the reward."

"Our procurement was successful, shall we say, but not without its own unique challenges. Although, I imagine you gathered that already. Miss Laurent had to negotiate her way out of a tight spot, and we ended up returning home on foot."

"Well then, where is this guest book? I must admit, I'm equally curious to find out what secrets it holds."

"You'd best find a distraction," Rex replied. "I was forced to hand the book over to Clark for safety while I went back to assist Miss Laurent. He'll bring it by today, but his idea of morning has very little to do with when the rooster crows and more to do with when the night owl settles in for a sleep."

Shortly after Dora and Inga joined them for breakfast, Clark made a surprise appearance. He entered the breakfast room looking much the worse for wear. His thick hair stood practically on end and even his moustache was in disarray. He slumped into the chair at the head of the table without asking first for permission.

Inga took one look at the man and asked the question that was on everyone's mind. "Have you been to bed at all?"

"Does sleeping on a bench in Hyde Park count?"

"In some social spheres, yes, but not ours. Given the circles under your eyes and the leaf stuck in your hair, I don't suggest you make a habit of it. Enough about your troubles. Where is the guest book?"

Clark jerked sideways and paled, nearly giving the rest of them a heart attack. But soon enough, he remembered what he had done with it. "I left it in the car, under the back seat. Rex, perhaps you be good enough to send one of the footman out to fetch it."

Rex nodded his approval, and the footman set off. In the meantime, Clark gratefully accepted a cup of coffee and Inga's offer to mix him a glass of her special hangover recovery tonic.

"I swear by them," Dora said, after Inga left for the kitchen. "Don't think too long or hard about the smell, and by all means, don't sip the concoction. Toss it back the same way you did the shots of rum last night and you'll be shipshape in no time."

It took Inga fifteen minutes to whip up the drink. The etched crystal did little to improve the appearance of the medication. Bands of brownish-green liquid swirled in the glass with every turn of the silver spoon. Inga pronounced it done and handed it to Clark with strict instructions to drink up.

Clark had the terrified face of a man on the eve of battle. He shrank in his seat and covered his mouth with his hands. Although he knew what he must do, but that didn't make the going any easier.

"Sooner you're over the breach, the sooner it's done, old chap," Rex said, nudging him along.

With all eyes on him, Clark tossed the drink back, wiped his mouth, and loosed a delicate belch. His face pinked, his eyes cleared, and he breathed a sigh of relief.

It wasn't to last. Within moments, Clark's face took on a greenish cast, and he scrambled from the room.

The Dowager Duchess glanced at Inga, worry evident in her raised eyebrows.

"It's all part of the process," Inga assured her. As if to underscore her lack of concern, she helped herself to another slice of buttered toast. "He'll be back shortly, feeling much more like himself. That level of toxin in the blood isn't good for anyone."

The dowager chuckled and shook her head, causing the pearls hanging from her ears to sway. "Miss Kay, I'm beginning to suspect that between you and Miss Laurent, you are the one we should be wary of."

"You're not wrong," Dora replied with a cheeky grin on her face. "If it isn't too forward of me to suggest, let's finish up so we can adjourn to the library and review our prize."

The dowager agreed. "The sooner we determine whether there is anything useful within the pages, the better. I fear that if we don't return the book to its rightful owner before nightfall, it may become impossible to avoid a scandal."

Rex flinched at his grandmother's words, but he noted Theodora seemed much less concerned. If the events of the prior evening weighed on her mind, she gave no sign of it.

He envied her lackadaisical attitude to life. Sure, he and his friends enjoyed a certain joie de vivre, but it was a frenetic one, borne of the knowledge that both life and their days of freedom from responsibility were short.

He continued to mull over the differences in their lives while they relocated to the family library. His grandmother instructed the footman where to set the guest book while Inga popped upstairs to retrieve the butler's journal.

"Set it here on the table," his grandmother said. "I'd offer to read, but I'd have to send the footman off for my glasses. Would one of you young people like to have the honour?"

"I'll do it," Dora answered. "Inga can sit beside me, to make referencing the dates and times easier."

"Excellent. We'll disperse ourselves across the other chairs. Rex, be a dear and check on Clark, will you? I'm certain he won't want to miss this."

Soon enough, they were all in their assigned places. Dora and Inga sat on one side, with the Dowager seated across from them. Rex sat at the head of the table while Clark chose to sit at the foot. He sank into the chair and rested his arms and head on the table, still not past the worst of his cure.

Rex covered his face in embarrassment while his grandmother blatantly ignored Clark's seating position.

"I bookmarked the relevant dates," Inga explained while flipping to the first marked page. "Check the Monday after Easter. Freddie went out mid-afternoon."

Rex leaned forward and watched as Dora turned the pages of the club guest book. From her composure, you'd never guess how much was riding on her response.

"Mid-afternoon, you say? That helps. Most of the guest arrivals are clustered around the mealtimes."

Rex couldn't stand the wait. He gave up the pretence of sitting back and rose from his chair. He tried leaning over, but all he accomplished was to block the light.

Dora gave him a sideways glance and scooted her chair over, making space for him to stand beside her. She skimmed her finger over the page, guiding them both as they mouthed the names.

"There!" Rex cried, reaching over to stop her hand. "Cavendish and Ponsonby."

Dora shook off Rex's hold on her hand. "Yes, yes, I see the names. Let's see who else was in attendance. Your grace, if you wouldn't mind taking notes." Dora rattled off a short list of men who arrived during a similar time frame. "Major Hobart is the last. What's the next date to check?"

Inga hurried to flip to the next day and Dora followed suit.

Rex's impatience continued to grow. "Look, there's Cavendish's name again."

"Yes, but Ponsonby is listed as another man's dinner guest." Dora pointed further down the page. "There are a couple of other names on here, including the Major, again. From what I can see, the man all but lives there."

The Dowager Duchess added the new names and put a tick next to the Major's listing. "My guess is Major Hobart is there most nights, given his lack of a wife or family. He probably considers it his home, which is why he's so up in arms about your unwelcome intrusion."

It turned out that Freddie visited White's three days in a row, each time with a different member playing host. Three visits garnered three names. That was more than enough to get them started. Rex's grandmother read them aloud. "Benedict Cavendish, Alan Neville, and Thomas Keppel. Each man hails from a well-respected family."

Her brow pinched with worry. "Rex, you can hardly go around questioning these men, particularly not if it sounds like you're accusing them of murder."

"She's right," Clark agreed, lifting his head from the table. "I know you don't come by this naturally, Rex, so let me offer you a word of advice. Before you go see anyone, come up with a cover story. Be prepared to prevaricate. And above all else, have some idea of what you hope to find out."

Rex blinked to clear his eyes, sure he had misheard his friend. "When did you get to be so clever?"

Clark was so affronted by the suggestion that he actually sat up. "Were you keeping me around for my looks? I've always been clever. How else do you think I come up with the themes for our scavenger hunts? And believe me, it requires a significant amount of fancy footwork and quick thinking to smooth feathers after our forays into unwelcome territory."

The Dowager Duchess intervened again, this time rising to her feet. "It sounds as though you have your work cut out. If Inga doesn't mind helping, I could use some assistance with penning a polite reply to Major Hobart that I can send along when we return the guest book. We'll leave the other three of you to search your memories for anything else that might be useful. With any luck, by nightfall you'll have come up with a starting point for the next stage of your investigation."

Chapter 18
Dora comes clean

Dora had plenty of experience with making difficult decisions. However, she was quickly coming to realise that none of it had prepared her for seeing her brother's name on a suspect list.

Benedict Cavendish, eldest son of the Duke of Dorset, had long been a thorn in Dora's side. A few years' older, Benedict had lorded his status as eldest son over the heads of her and her brother Wills. He gave orders and expected them to be followed.

Dora and Wills had minds of their own. Tweaking their priggish brother's nose became their favourite hobby, especially since it was remarkably easy. The more he chided them for misbehaving, the worse hooligans they became.

It would absolutely horrify Benedict to discover that he was partially responsible for Dora's decision to leave her life as Lady Dorothy Cavendish and become Theodora Laurent.

Wait. Scratch *would be* and make that *was*. Contempt had been writ large in his expression after he grabbed a hold of Dora during her attempted escape the night before. She'd muttered the same words she'd used dozens of times as a child and watched as realisation struck him dead between the eyes.

His expression had shifted into a rictus of horror as he beheld his baby sister. Not only grown, but flashy and notorious to boot. She was his worst nightmare up and walking in the world.

But that didn't make him a killer. Benedict Cavendish would never dirty his hands by killing someone, nor would he arrange for someone's death. No matter how many years had passed since their childhood days in the nursery, Dora knew what lay at the centre of his heart.

Honour. Loyalty. Respect.

He'd sooner off himself than do anything that might tarnish the family name. So why had Freddie met with Benedict?

Rex and Clark both stared off into space, likely asking themselves the same question.

There was no way Freddie was aware of her connection to Benedict. In fact, given Benedict's reaction to seeing her in the flesh, she was confident Benedict didn't know anything about how she'd really spent the years after the war.

Benedict thought the same thing as the rest of the world. Lady Dorothy Cavendish, newly widowed Viscountess of Lisle, had retired to an estate in the French countryside to spend the rest of her days mourning the husband she'd lost.

With that cover story in place, Dora had been freed to explore the world as Theodora Laurent. Undercover and unencumbered, Dora rubbed shoulders with the world elite, gathering information for the British government all along the way. Despite the importance of her work, Dora felt sure Benedict wouldn't smile at her choices.

It was only a matter of time before he marched into this very room and demanded an explanation. To keep Rex and the others from finding out her secret, Dora had dispatched Harris this morning with a message for her brother. She'd promised to visit within twenty-four hours with an explanation.

She didn't intend to show up with Rex and Clark in tow. That meant she had to turn their minds in a different direction. Someone else's name had to rise to the top of the list.

Dora watched Rex's cat thread a careful path between the objets d'art displayed on a nearby shelf. She understood the challenge, feeling herself as though she were an ancient Greek mariner sailing between Scylla and Charybdis. If she strayed too far one way, Rex and Clark might uncover her secret. Too far in the other direction and they'd end up stumbling into a world of spies.

If the cat could do it, so could she. Dora snapped her fingers and called the cat. "Mews, come cuddle with me."

The cat's ears perked, and it did as was told. Or almost, anyway. Mews pranced across the room, weaving between the chair legs, and leapt into Rex's lap. Rex set to work scratching the cat's fluffy ears. Dora swore the cat scowled at her, making its allegiance known.

She knew what she had to do. She had to guide Rex and Clark into figuring out Freddie was conducting an investigation. The whys and hows weren't to be shared, but with a deft hand, Dora was confident she could constrain their path and keep them moving in a safe direction.

"Dear me, this is quite the quandary," she said, shattering the silence. "Does anyone else feel as though they're reading one of Conan Doyle's tales?"

"More like acting the lead parts. I lay claim to Holmes," Clark replied, flashing her a debonair smile despite his dishevelled state. "Would you care to be my Watson?"

Rex rolled his eyes and muttered for Clark to stop. Still stroking the cat, Rex asked Dora a question. "Why do you say that now? I told you Freddie's death was no accident. What made you decide it is a proper mystery?"

"Pass me the list," Dora said, holding out a hand. She took the paper and skimmed the names. "Three meetings, each with a different man, and all within a day of one another. Isn't it obvious? Freddie must have been investigating something."

Clark's mouth dropped open, but Rex displayed little surprise. "I was quickly reaching the same conclusion. As I told you both, Freddie was up to something. Now, more than ever, I believe he had discovered... something. Damned if I can figure out what."

"You have a point there, old chap. If Freddie was running any sort of investigation or search, why wouldn't Freddie have asked us for help?" Clark asked. "Or gone to the police, for that matter?"

"Who's to say he didn't intend to do just that, but was killed before he could tell anyone what he'd found? I hate to say it, but it's equally possible that he did approach the police or someone in power and they refused to listen. Look at us now! Isn't that where we've found ourselves?"

Dora knew Rex was wrong. The people in power were fully cognisant of the situation, and had tasked Dora to ferret out the truth. But now wasn't the time to raise that point. Based on the serious expressions on their faces, the men were close to embracing wholeheartedly the idea that Freddie had been investigating something. Rex's mouth had a grim set to it.

Only Clark was hesitating. He stared off into the distance, smoothing his moustache while he turned the question over in his mind.

She had to push Clark over the line. She shifted uncomfortably in her seat, looking ill at ease for the first time in a long while. When Clark cast an eye her way, she nibbled on her lip and fluttered her lashes.

"Please don't hate me for waiting to admit this. I probably should have told you this earlier, but until now, I'd discounted my intuition."

Both men stared at her, wearing matching expressions of raised eyebrows and frowns. "Go on," Rex said, waving his hand. "No time like the present to come clean."

Dora let the moment stretch before finally taking a deep breath and diving in. "Remember when we ventured out to the pub, and I told you what the barmaid said?"

Rex and Clark both stilled, as though bracing for whatever she said next.

"I think she lied. I think Freddie was there to spy on someone, but not for the reason she said."

"I knew it!" Rex said and slammed his hand onto the table. "That story had to be a fabrication. We lived with Freddie for years, first in school and then during the war. If he'd had any proclivities, we'd have known about them."

"On that, I agree," Clark chimed in.

"Thank goodness! This has been weighing on my mind ever since, and I'm so relieved you both agree." Dora picked up the notepad and turned to a new page. With her pen in hand, she suggested they start a second list. "Assuming we're on the right track, that means that Freddie somehow got from White's to the Ten Bells. I can't begin to imagine how anyone's paths would take them to both of those venues, but let's assume they did. That means we need to know more about the pub." She wrote the name and location. "Rex, you played cards with some regulars. Was there anything about them that stuck out? Did they talk about their jobs or any social activities?"

"Err," Rex glanced upwards as he searched his memory. "They smelled like seawater and rotten fish, and most of their jokes had a nautical theme. I'd say they were either sailors or dockworkers."

Dora added more notes and then retrieved the original page. "Of the men that Freddie met at White's — Benedict Cavendish, Alan Neville, and Thomas Keppel — do any of them have a connection to the sea? Either through their family history, or their investments?"

"Cavendish is a yes, but that doesn't mean much," added Clark. "His family's investment portfolio would rival the Crown's."

"Keppel is a better bet. His family made their fortune as an early investor in the East India Company. When it dissolved, they set up their own shipping line. In fact, my father uses Keppel's ships to move our whiskey from Ireland to the warehouse near the Thames. You know the one I mean." Rex gave Dora a sly glance, causing her to giggle.

Clark eyed the pair, but rightly guessed he'd get no explanation. "Speaking of warehouses, doesn't Neville own a large swath of real estate near the docklands?"

"He does. How did I forget? Neville also happens to be on friendly terms with Lord Cavendish. It doesn't require one to stretch the imagination to pull together a picture. Freddie went to Cavendish first, for whatever reason. Cavendish could have sent him to Neville. If his concerns were more on the sea-based than land, Keppel was the logical progression."

"Hold on, I'm writing all this down," Dora said. She took her time penning the names, using the quiet to decide her next step. Letting him speak with Benedict was out of the question. Her instincts screamed that Neville was the safest bet.

No sooner did the thought coalesce in her mind, than Rex laid his hands on the table and made his own pronouncement. "I'm going to pay a call to Keppel."

"Is it wise to skip ahead?" she countered. "What if Keppel is the one who killed Freddie? We should start with Neville. Do either of you know him well?"

"I've seen him at soirees a time or two," Clark said. "That probably isn't much help."

"It will have to be," Dora replied. "Last night, we found security in numbers. I suggest we do the same again. Send him an invitation to join us for dinner."

"Tonight?" Rex shook his head. "There's no way he'll be available on such short notice. Not to mention, I doubt my grandmother will appreciate making your presence known more widely than it already is."

Dora brushed a lock of hair from her face and fluffed her bob. "You forget, there's another house available to us. If you dangle me as bait, he'll make himself free. After all, no matter where you look in London, there's no one more scintillating than little old me."

"You're not suggesting..."

"Yes, I am. We can sneak into my home and out again through the back entrance. Other than my servants, no one will be the wiser."

Clark rubbed his palms together. "Miss Laurent, tell your staff to set an intimate table for four. There's no way I'm missing out on this."

"As if I'd leave you off the list!" Dora made her excuses, explaining that she and Inga would need to get to work on the dinner. "I'll leave it to you chaps to handle the invite and the dinner table conversation."

"You can count on us," Rex assured her.

Dora sincerely hoped that was true. Despite her devil-may-care approach to life, whipping up a dinner party fit for the beau monde on a few hours' notice was hardly child's play. Especially when you factored in the need for some rather unique cocktails.

With Inga's help, Dora was sure she could mix up a recipe that would leave the men as languid as putty and desperate for a good night's rest. With Rex and Clark out of the way, she'd be free to pay a midnight call on her dear brother.

Living a double life was not for the faint of heart. But as a trill of excitement ran along her spine, Dora knew it was pointless denying the truth. Even if she could go back in time, she wouldn't have her life be any other way.

Chapter 19
Dinner with Neville

Rex waited in the car while Clark left to collect Neville. After his previous brush with a speeding bullet, it would be a long while before Rex was comfortable parking his car in plain sight. Case in point, at the moment he was idling in an alleyway a few minutes' walk from where Neville lived. Rather than drive his all-to-recognisable Rolls-Royce, he'd opted for a lower profile pitch-black Oxford 'bullnose' Morris.

Rex wished he knew what to expect from the evening. His grandmother had shared what little insight she had into Neville's character. She referred to him as having the personality of a little puppy. What did that even mean?

Rex tried to square the image of a grown man in his thirties with the rambunctious young hounds his family used for their hunts. The resulting picture was so ridiculous that he laughed out loud. Fortunately, Clark appeared with Neville a step behind, saving him from further tumbling down that rabbit hole.

As soon as Rex laid eyes on Neville, he understood what his grandmother had met. The man did not stride, walk, plod, or stumble. He bounced on the balls of his feet, showing a boisterous enthusiasm uncommon in the upper class.

It wasn't only his movements that made Rex think of his hounds. Neville had the same brown eyes that flitted from side to side in excitement. He was short for an Englishman, but still had long, skinny legs that ate up the ground with every step.

Neville spotted Rex waiting in the car and a broad smile engulfed his face, lighting up his features. In his enthusiasm, he burbled on; the words tumbling from his mouth before he was even inside the car. "Lord Rex, I can't tell you how delighted I am to be included on one of your infamous excursions. All Clark would tell me was that I'd hate myself forever if I didn't agree to clear my diary."

"I may have oversold this. I wasn't expecting Neville to be so enthusiastic," Clark confessed, wiggling his eyebrows at Rex.

Rex turned in his seat to glance behind and found himself nearly nose to nose with Neville. The man was sitting as far forward as the space would allow, with his elbows resting on the back of the front seat so that he wouldn't miss a single word. Rex quickly shifted backwards to give himself breathing room.

"Welcome, Neville. And please, call me Rex. We appreciate you making yourself available on such short notice."

Neville waved off the thanks. "Think nothing of it, old chap. Ever since my mother declared me to be on the hunt for a bride, I've spent my days and nights having awkward conversations with young women barely out of the schoolroom. This, at least, promises to be an evening free of any expectations of marriage."

Clark snorted. "You do not know how true those words are. Rex, do you want to tell Neville where we're taking him?"

"You didn't?" Rex asked. He dared another glance at their passenger. "You agreed to come along with no idea of what we have in store for the evening?"

Neville shrugged. "As I said, anything is better than another debutante ball. Besides, when else will I get an opportunity to join you? If I were a decade younger and still footloose like you men, I'd give you both a run for your money. But alas, I've got responsibility riding like a monkey on my shoulder. Tonight is all I have, and I mean to make the most of it. I'm in your hands. Don't let me down."

Letting Neville down was the least of Rex's worries. Failing to identify Freddie's killer... now that was an entirely different matter.

"We aim to please," Rex declared, revving the engine. "But I won't say more than that. It will be far more fun to see your face once we arrive."

Rex kept to a sedate pace while traversing the city and soon pulled into the alley behind Dora's Belgravia abode. Using their agreed upon signal, Rex squeezed the rubber bulb to sound his horn twice in rapid succession. Within moments, the gates swung open to reveal Harris, Theodora's butler.

"By Jove, is the man wearing a chequered vest under his coat?" Neville asked. Rather than disapproving, his voice had the high pitch of excitement.

"Steady on," Clark chided. "You've not seen the half of it."

Indeed, Neville's eyes were wide and unblinking when they walked into the rear garden. An impressive shade tree stood in the centre of the space, providing cover for languid afternoon picnics. In the far back corner was a summerhouse painted sky blue. A single lantern hung from its ceiling, casting light upon a chaise longue covered in cushions. Rex's mind was happy to fill his mind with visions of how he and Theodora could put that space to good use. It took all his willpower to hurry on.

Finally, they arrived at the entrance to Dora's conservatory. There, amidst the brightly coloured spring blossoms of geraniums and Delphiniums, sat Theodora, looking like a rose in full bloom. She was overdressed for the occasion in a sleeveless black dress with pale pink floral appliqués across the Georgette bodice and beaded fringe dancing at the knee. She took a puff from her long-handled cigarette and blew a perfect ring of smoke into the air.

Neville missed a step, and only Rex's quick thinking allowed him to avoid a tumble. He recovered admirably enough and rushed ahead to take Dora's outstretched hand. He dropped to one knee and pressed a kiss to the top of her hand. "Miss Laurent, this is truly an unexpected honour."

"The pleasure is all mine," Dora said in a breathy voice, rising from her seat. "Apologies for the unusual arrival point. I seem to have acquired an over-eager admirer who is determined to take out the competition."

"Am I competition?" Neville asked, before his brain could catch up with his mouth.

Rex snickered into his hand and quickly covered it with a cough.

Dora, however, wasn't in the least put off by his blatantly inappropriate question. "Look around, Lord Neville. There are three of you now, but who's to say which one of you will still be standing at night's end."

Clark bumped Neville aside and offered Dora his arm. "Neville can stand around all he wants. It's the lying down part that I'm dreaming of."

Dora's laughter trilled through the air like bird song, rendering the peaceful atmosphere of her conservatory complete. "Lord Clark, you are a gas! Come inside and get a cocktail. My butler has a new recipe you absolutely must taste to believe."

They left Rex to follow behind, with Neville in tow. Rex reminded him, "Your mother will never ever approve of her, man. Best to keep your wits about you lest you find yourself rushed to the altar."

"If it's with Theodora Laurent, I'll go to my destiny with nary a complaint."

Rex shook his head. There was no helping Neville. The puppy was smitten. There'd be no getting anything of significance out of the man, not while he was this far gone. Rex worried that they'd misplayed their hands, and would walk away with nothing to guide their search for the truth of what happened to Freddie.

As the night went on, Rex's opinion of the situation shifted from one of concern to pure admiration. Yes, Neville was ever more enthralled by Theodora. He practically hung from each word she uttered, and would have gratefully lapped up crumbs by her feet.

For her part, Theodora never lost control of the conversation. She coaxed his entire life story from his lips, with him nary the wiser to her tactics.

And tactics, they were.

Rex had spent enough time at the front lines of the war to recognise a strategist when he saw one. Anytime Neville clammed up or grew reticent, she'd lean forward and beg for more, showing a hint of cleavage and an inviting smile. She used every tool in her vast arsenal of appeal to learn what she needed.

Through it all, Rex never grew bored. It was testament to Theodora's deft hand at the conversation. She'd ask a few questions of Neville, find a connection to Clark, and before Rex knew it, he was chiming in. Between the rich food and fine wine, Rex's demeanour grew ever more languid. When the butler brought dessert, he nearly declined. However, the heady smell of pineapple gave him second thoughts.

"I simply adore pineapple upside down cake," Dora cooed while spooning a generous portion of whipped cream onto her plate. "To think, this delectable treat was once considered a luxury item. It was so scarce on Britain's shores that the hoity toity crowd would rent one for display, and never dare to slice into it. Now, one simply has to pop down to the market and pineapples are there for the taking. I suppose we have you, in part, to thank for this, Lord Neville."

"Me?" Neville whipped his gaze up from his dessert plate.

"Aren't you somehow involved in shipping?" Dora asked.

"Only the tail end of the venture," Neville replied. "My family invested in the docks years ago. Ask me anything you want about ships coming into port, but don't expect much about the journeys they take to get there."

Rex leapt at the invitation. What started as a fishing expedition to see what Freddie might have asked quickly turned into an education into England's import system. While he'd thought himself well-versed, Rex soon discovered that his knowledge wouldn't fill a thimble compared to Neville. Everything from determining which imports could be stored together to ensuring produce and meats moved straight from boat to train was all new to Rex.

By the time their dessert plates were clean and wineglasses empty, Rex's mind was reeling from everything he'd learned. Before that moment, he'd have sworn that his education had been excellent. Now, he was painfully aware of exactly how limited it had been. His desire to scratch below the surface and discover just how much more it took to keep society fed and clothed rose until it clawed at his nerves, encouraging him to go in search of a book or tutor.

Neville, however, had no idea of the profound impact he'd had. He took in the wide eyes and dumbfounded stares around the table and apologised. "Blimey! You asked a simple question and I've talked your ears off. I hope you'll forgive my eagerness to prattle on about my favourite subject. Truth be told, I get so few opportunities. Other than the three of you and Freddie Ponsonby, no one has asked me anything about my work in years."

"Freddie asked you about shipping?" Dora asked breezily, barely hinting at her interest.

"Huh? Oh yes, strange thing that," Neville replied. "He asked if we could chat and I invited him to White's. He peppered me with questions about how illegal trade works... about how someone could import drugs, guns... you know. Speaking frankly, the conversation made me uncomfortable."

"My word, I should think so. As happy as I am to walk on the wilder side of society, there are limits to what is acceptable." Dora searched the faces of the men around the table. "Lord Clark and Lord Rex, you were friends with Freddie for much longer than I was. Did either of you have an inkling about this?"

The men were as mystified as she was. The silence didn't last long. Neville jumped in with a reassurance. "I was concerned, as I'm sure you can imagine. Freddie said a friend was in over their heads, and he wanted to help them out. But to do that, he needed a better understanding of the illicit trade."

Rex caught his breath. Could this be the clue they needed to make sense of everything? Without hesitation, he blurted his question, "What friend?"

"No idea," Neville answered. "But my gut said he was telling the truth. I didn't pry." He reached across the table to get his wineglass. He drank deep, lost in his own thoughts.

Rex watched Neville's expression shift as he put the pieces together.

"Wait a minute. Is that why you asked me here? But, how would you know..." Neville's voice trailed off, and he wrinkled his brow. "Dear God! Is that why you lot lifted the guest book from the club last night?"

For a moment, Rex worried that Neville was going to get angry. Instead, the man threw back his head and laughed.

"All this time, I assumed your forays into petty crime were

the product of boredom. Now I see the truth! You're not entertaining yourselves. You're gathering information."

Clark spoke before Rex could get a word in. "You give us far too much credit, old chap. Ninety-nine per cent of the time our antics are nothing more than boredom-busters. This was the very rare one per cent where they were not. But how did you hear about the theft so quickly?"

"Surely you jest! Women barrelled their way into our inner sanctum, and our secret tome of attendees went missing. The club owners were livid and looking for someone to blame. There's not a member of White's whose ears weren't ringing this morning."

"Oh, dear me," Dora said. She bit her lip, playing the role of apologetic prankster to perfection. "It's my fault, so let me explain. I mentioned earlier about my trouble with an ardent admirer. I worry the same man might have been responsible for Freddie's untimely death, but I do not know who he is. I asked Lord Rex and Lord Clark for help to figure it out. But now you've said Freddie was asking about illegal activities at the dock and I have no clue anymore what to think."

Rex felt the same, not that he could say that out loud. What friend was Freddie helping? They ran in similar social circles. If someone in their set was in debt to the gangs, or otherwise caught up in something that big, surely he'd have known? Rex struggled to form a picture in his mind, but the connections were still far too ethereal to come together.

Rex wiped his face with his hands, feeling the days since Freddie's demise stacking like bricks on his back. He glanced up in time to catch Neville yawning. The hour was late. A night of sleep was what they all needed. They could regroup again come morning.

Rex folded his napkin and set it beside his plate. "Miss Laurent, I hate to eat and run, but I fear an evening in your presence is more than this mere mortal can survive... let alone two in a row."

"I must agree," Clark chimed in. "And not just because you're giving me a lift back home. What say you, Neville?"

Neville gave a heavy sigh and admitted he was in the same boat. "I do hope you'll allow me to call on you again, Miss Laurent. Next time, I'll play the role of inquisitor and you can tell me all about yourself."

Dora promised to let him do just that and accompanied them back the way they came. Rex motioned for Clark and Neville to go ahead of him, and lingered for a moment.

"Will you return to Grandmama's tonight?"

Dora shook her head. "I'm safe enough indoors. We'll keep the curtains drawn tight, and Harris will be on guard should anyone dare try to sneak in. I'll come for you tomorrow and we can determine with whom to speak next."

Rex knew a dismissal when he heard one, but something compelled him to stay where he was. Moonlight flowed through the glass ceiling of the conservatory, casting Dora in a pale glow. Her red-blonde hair glittered above the deep green pools of her eyes.

Dora lifted a hand and offered it to him. "Goodnight, Rex."

Heaven help him. Rex took her hand in his, feeling the delicate touch of her silky fingers on his palm and smelling the perfume on her wrist. His gaze never dropped from her eyes while he lifted her hand and brushed a kiss across her wrist. "Until morning, Theodora."

Chapter 20
A warm family welcome

Dora stood utterly still in her conservatory, watching until Rex disappeared from sight and then listening for the sound of Harris closing the gate behind him. She told herself that she was merely being careful and making sure no one saw the men leave. However, that didn't explain why she continued to run her thumb over the place where Rex had kissed her.

"Everything all right?" Harris asked when he came in and spied her standing there.

Dora gave a start but quickly covered by flowing into motion. "Two sets of eyes are better than one," she said in explanation. "They stayed later than I expected, and I learned less than I hoped. I'm left to cross my fingers that my dearest brother will have more light to shed on the matter."

"You'll have to hurry if you want to get there before midnight," Harris reminded her.

As if to prove Harris's point, the clock atop the nearby church tolled the eleventh hour. The ringing of the bell catapulted Dora into action. She fled back into the house and up the stairs to her boudoir. There, she found Inga waiting with her nighttime costume in hand.

For the rare occasions when Dora was forced to venture out under the cover of nightfall, she'd procured a pair of black men's trousers, a forest green shirt and a lightweight, black cotton scarf. A black flat cap completed the disguise. The combination of colours and fabrics ensured she could just as easily hide in the shadows as amongst the branches of a tree.

"I think you should take Harris inside with you." Inga said. "Benedict is your brother, but we do not know how he is going to act."

Dora gave a bleak laugh and shook her head. "No, this is something I have to do on my own. That Harris will wait nearby is all the reassurance I need. As you rightly noted, Benedict is family. No matter how angry he is, I am positive he won't harm me."

Inga stepped into Dora's path, blocking her from leaving the room. "Harm? I'm concerned he'll decide that locking you up and throwing away the key is the best way to keep you out of further trouble."

In reply, Dora leaned over and slid a dagger from the inside of the boot. She lifted it up and held it so than Inga could see it. "If I lived the life of a normal titled English lady, he might get away with that. I almost hope he tries so that he can learn whom he is up against. I am his sister, but I'm far from a baby."

Inga flattened her lips into a grim line, but let the conversation end there. She stepped aside and allowed Dora to head off on her own.

Harris was waiting beside a black sedan. It was nothing to crow about, but that was part of the allure. In fact, this car was one of the first purchases Dora had made upon her arrival in England. As soon as she realised just how many of them filled the streets, she sent Harris out to buy a used automobile from one of the taxi companies. The rundown appearance ensured no one gave it a second look.

Harris surveyed her appearance with a critical eye and gave her cap a tug to better shadow her face. "You'll do. I'll wait in the car. If you don't come out after an hour, I'm coming in."

"You'll do no such thing, at least not before dawn. Benedict and I will have much to discuss."

"Lucky for me, then, that I've got a flask of coffee to keep me awake. Let's get a move on."

The drive to Benedict's home took hardly any time at all. Dora didn't have to think twice about how to get inside. He lived in the family home. Despite the years that had passed, she could still picture the grounds perfectly.

True to his word, Harris parked a few houses down, choosing a spot in the shadows between two street lamps. Dora gave his arm a quick squeeze and then climbed out over the door, making nary a sound.

She surveyed the garden wall. The limbs of the old beech tree were still there, waiting with outstretched arms to help the wayward Cavendish children sneak in and out of the garden.

Dora used the familiar hand and toeholds in the stone wall to reach the thickest branch. Her hands and feet had grown larger since the last time she'd made this trek, but somehow she made it work. Once in the tree, she slithered across the branch until she was within reach of a window on the second floor of the house. She crossed her fingers and then gave it a gentle shove, hoping no one had fixed the broken latch.

The window slid up, but gave a groan of protest that had her swearing. With Wills dead all these years, and her off on her own, there'd been no one there to oil the tread. She hurried inside and tiptoed to the door, not even needing the moonlight to find her way between the furniture.

Dora put her ear to the door and held still, listening for any sounds. Only silence. Encouraged, she twisted the handle and pulled the door open. She barely had time to set foot on the hallway runner before she heard her brother's voice.

"Bloody hell, it really is you."

"Language, Benedict," Dora chastised, waving her finger at her brother. "What would Mama say if she heard that word coming from your lips?"

"Our mother grew up on a horse farm in Virginia. I imagine she's heard worse. Besides, given the circumstances, I'm sure she'd have choice words of her own."

Dora crossed her arms over her chest and refused to let her brother goad her. Looking at him, now grown, was like seeing her childhood memory of her father. He was a chip off the old block, in every sense of the words. Same cunning smile, cleft chin, and thick brows. But where her father had a soft edge, Benedict was all hard planes. Father had Mother to blunt the worst of his anger. Benedict, unmarried and alone, had no one to do the same.

At least Dora knew what she was up against. She leaned against the wooden door frame and cocked up an eyebrow. "Are you going to invite me down to the study for a drink, or do you mean to hold this inquisition in the hallway?"

Benedict rolled his eyes at her and turned, marching off without a backwards glance. Dora followed him down the main staircase, around the corner, and into the only lit room on the ground floor. At first glance, the study was the same as ever. However, as Dora walked deeper into the room, she began to notice the subtle changes.

The landscape over the fireplace was new, a field in Provence instead of the old racing scene. The desk was the same, as was the chair, but the seating area boasted more modern furnishings with cleaner lines and less fuss.

The rumours were true. Her parents had retired to the country estate, leaving Benedict in charge of the city matters.

Those matters didn't include her, regardless of what he might think.

The lone glass of amber liquor sitting atop the desk told Dora that Benedict had a head start. He circled the heavy antique and took his place, watching for her to follow the unspoken command.

Start as you mean to go on, Dora thought. She ignored his weighty glare and helped herself to a drink from the drinks table. Glass in hand, she walked past the visitor chair and went for the sofa instead. Although the piece wasn't the same, she chose the cushion closest to the window. In the daylight, it would provide a direct view of the garden on the other side of the window. She had, however, far more interest in watching the man hard at work inside. She'd spent hours in that spot, reading quietly while her father dealt with his own responsibilities.

Benedict was forced to turn his chair so he could look her in the face. Good. He was on the back foot and the battle of wits had barely begun.

"I'm waiting," he hissed.

"For what? Dawn? A refill? This is your home. You hardly need to ask permission before getting a drink."

"For an explanation," he huffed. His face was flushed and his mouth frozen in a moue of disapproval. "You are supposed to be living in France, grieving over your dead husband, not cavorting around London, masquerading under an assumed name while living as a loose woman with fast friends."

Dora sipped her Scotch, letting the liquid burn slide down the back of her throat and warm her middle. With one sentence, Benedict had conveyed more than he'd intended. Her parents were aware she wasn't living in France. They didn't know much else, but she'd made Lord Audley tell them that much. The last thing any of them could afford was for her parents to pay a surprise visit. Yet, they hadn't seen fit to pass that tidbit along to Benedict.

Dora didn't need to ask why. Benedict would have never approved. Even now, seeing her a woman grown, he was calling her onto the carpet like a naughty child in need of a scolding. She would not dance to his tune. She ignored his question and gave an instruction of her own.

"Freddie Ponsonby. You spoke with him at the club. Tell me what you discussed."

Benedict's brows shot upward. "Is that what this is about? Your lover shot dead in some back alley. Oh yes, I learned all about the two of you. Twenty-four hours is more than enough time for me to read through the previous editions of the paper. Theodora Laurent, they call you. I should have known. You were always pretending to be Empress Theodora instead of playing dolls like normal girls."

"Some women dream of raising a family. I had every intention of ruling part of the world. I still do, albeit differently than what I imagined." Dora sighed, feeling much older than her twenty-four years. She didn't want to argue like children. "It's been a decade since Mother shipped me off to finishing school. Ten years since we last laid eyes on one another, Benedict. Despite what you think, I don't owe you my history. Like you—like Wills—I spent time at the front lines. Wills gave his life for our country. I've given mine. Do not presume to think you know anything about my choices."

Invoking the name of their brother was a risky gamble. Wills had always stood between them, both in age order and in keeping the peace. With him gone, there was no longer anyone to blunt the edges of Benedict's temper or rein in Dora's worst impulses.

Still, the gambit worked. Benedict's clenched fists loosened and the colour in his cheeks receded. He reached over, grabbed his glass, and took a deep pull. By the time he'd swallowed the liquor, he was once again in control.

"Have you told Mother and Father that you're here?"

"No one knows my real identity, and it must remain that way. Consider it a state secret, if you must. But to answer your real question, I do intend to contact them once things have quieted. And on my own terms," she hastened to add. "Now, answer a question of mine. Freddie. What did the two of you discuss?"

"Investments."

"You can do better than that. The man had three conversations in short order and ended up murdered. As far as I can tell, the first conversation was with you. It's justice I seek, not blame. So please, elaborate."

Benedict shook his head. "Why? So you can end up being the next corpse they find?"

"So I can avoid stumbling into whatever situation Freddie found himself in. I've already spoken with Alan Neville. I know Freddie was after information on the illicit trade that runs through the docks. What I don't know is why he needed that information." Dora took a deep breath and steadied her voice. "Won't you help me? Was it you he was helping?"

Benedict reared back as though he'd be slapped. "Me? Of course, he wasn't helping me. I don't know what you are talking about."

Dora held her brother's gaze, but softened enough to let a hint of her anguish shine through. His shoulders slumped. She had him.

"If what you say is true, I'm more worried about you than ever. I spoke honestly. Freddie came to me asking for advice. He said he had come into a small amount of funds and was keen to invest in trade, either incoming or export. He asked who within our circle would be the best to guide his decision. I mentioned Neville's name, and one other."

"Keppel," Dora said, filling in the blank.

"Yes, that's the one. I wasn't close with Freddie, but I'm still sorry he's gone. We lost far too many from our generation as it is. I won't ask much, because you won't listen, but, Dora, you need to let this go. It would kill Mother to lose another child, to say nothing of the guilt I'd carry." Benedict leaned forward and looked her in the eyes. "Leave matters to the professionals."

Dora tossed back the rest of her drink and set the empty glass on the nearby table. She stood and waved for Benedict to keep his seat. Before she left the room, she made her parting words. "You still don't understand. You say to leave it to the professionals. Darling brother, that's exactly what I am."

Chapter 21
An accident goes awry

The streets were eerily empty at this late hour. Without the bustle of other automobiles or pedestrians to distract them from their thoughts, Rex, Clark, and Neville rode in a pensive silence.

Rex knew they were all thinking about the same thing without needing to ask.

Freddie.

Every new piece of information they learned added little more than another nebulous thread. What Rex needed was something to tie them all together. He hated to admit it, even to himself, but his hopes rested on speaking with Keppel.

A flash of light caught Rex's eye and pulled his mind back to the present. He pressed on the brake to slow the car.

"Why are you slowing down? My house is after the next intersection," Clark asked from the back seat.

"I know where you live. There's been an accident," Rex replied. His headlights illuminated the scene, revealing a delivery lorry parked at an angle and a shadow lying in front of the vehicle.

Neville leaned sideways to get a better view, practically

panting into Rex's ear. "Should we stop to help? It must have just happened." Neville gasped and added, "My word! Is that a man lying in the street?"

"We have no choice but to stop. The vehicle is blocking our way." Rex allowed the car to slow even further until it coasted to a stop on the side of the street a few yards from the scene. The top of the car was already down, so they waited inside while a man approached from the pavement.

There was something vaguely familiar about the man's shape, but he was pointing a flashlight in Rex's eyes, preventing him from getting a good look.

"We could use some 'elp," the man said in a gruff voice. "Do you mind?"

Rex exchanged glances with Neville and Clark. Both men shrugged and moved to get out of the car. They met in front of Rex's car and followed the man as he guided them closer to the accident scene.

"There's a taxi stuck on the other side," he explained. He sped up, circling around the back of the lorry.

Neville and Clark picked up their pace. Rex did not. His instincts shouted that something was wrong, but he couldn't figure out what it was. Perhaps it was simply the late hour and the drink they'd enjoyed that was making him feel out of sorts. He took a deep breath of the bracing night air to clear his head, and that's when it hit him.

There was no lingering scent of burnt tyres or spilled petrol, both hallmarks of an automobile accident. He rushed to catch up with his friends. He barely made it past the rear of the lorry before a screech caught his ear.

Rex turned back in time to see the rear gate of the lorry bed swing open. A group of men leapt to the ground, holding heavy wooden clubs in their hands. Rex clenched his hands into fists and readied himself for a fight, but the sound of someone saying his name halted him in his tracks.

He spun around and found himself face to face with the ruffian. He recognised the sunburnt cheeks and crooked nose from the pub. Arnie... that was his name.

Arnie's eyes widened in recognition. "You're Lord Rex? Of course, you are. You've been causing a lot of trouble. My guv'nor asked us to send you on a holiday. We can do this the easy way or the 'ard way."

"Easy way!" Clark shouted before Rex could get out a word. "We've got no plans for the rest of the week. And, who wouldn't want to go on a holiday?"

Arnie threw back his head and laughed. "Listen to 'em talk, boys. Bet they won't sing that tune come mornin'? 'elp the gents into the lorry, will ya, Gord?"

Gord approached, carrying black clothes under his arm. He stopped in front of Rex and pulled one loose. When he shook it out, Rex realised it was a bag. Gord motioned for him to lean over, and then he slipped the bag over Rex's head.

"Tie up their 'ands, boys, and then 'elp 'em inside."

Rex held his hands out front, making it easier for the other brute to wrap a rope around his wrists. With further manhandling, the kidnappers lifted the three upper-class gentlemen and shoved them into a seated position on the lorry bed.

The lorry's engine turned over a few times before it caught. Rex hunched over, doing his best to remain upright, when the lorry took off. In the limited space, he bumped against Neville and Clark. He tried shifting the other way and caught a kick in his ribs for his efforts. After that, he decided he was better off holding still, even if the bumpy ride made his teeth chatter.

Neville wasn't as bright. The hood muffled his voice, but the words were loud enough to be heard. "Where are you taking us? And why me? I think there's been a mistake!"

Gord's voice interrupted Neville's laments. "You're asking too many questions, mate. Why don't you catch a few winks on the way?"

Sleep was the last thing Rex intended to do, but a whack atop the head settled the matter for him.

* * *

Rex dragged in a breath and ended up with a mouthful of smelly cotton instead. In a mad panic, he clawed at the fabric covering his face. His hands moved in unison, the wrists still bound with an itchy rope. He moved the fabric covering his face enough to get a glimpse of light and a rush of clean air.

The combination eased the panic closing in his throat. He rolled over and barely bit back a yelp when he bumped up against something, hitting a tender spot on the back of his skull.

The pain brought clarity. He remembered.

There'd been an accident, or a staged one, anyway. Arnie and Gord from the Ten Bells had been there, lying in wait for Rex to pass. But how had they known when and where to catch him?

His head hurt something fierce, and wracking his brain with more questions was only making it worse. He felt around in the air above his head, checking for other impediments. Finding none, he pushed himself into a sitting position and finally worked the cloth bag free from his head. He inhaled again, filling his lungs with air, and coughed as the rancid taste of spoilt fish burnt the back of his throat.

He wrinkled his nose and looked around. He was in a warehouse. Neville and Clark were there too, both still knocked out cold. He took in his surroundings, making note of each detail. The skylights were caked with dirt, but enough light came through to confirm it was past dawn.

Other than the squawk of gulls, the cavernous room was silent. Every movement Rex made echoed, yet no one had come to check on him.

He suspected they were alone.

From what he could tell, they had unceremoniously dumped Rex and his friends in an uncluttered area in the middle of a crowded warehouse. To his left, towers of battered crates and broken timber filled the space, casting strange shadows against the walls and floor. The crates and boxes to his right were in decidedly better condition. Rex scooted across the floor, somewhat disadvantaged by his bound hands. He prodded Neville until the man roused from sleep.

"Wake up," he hissed, while pulling the hood from Neville's head. "It's me, Rex."

Neville blinked slowly, bleary-eyed in the pale morning light. While he came to, Rex freed Clark from his head covering and shook him awake.

"Where are we?" Clark asked, his voice thick with sleep.

"I'm hoping Neville can tell us," Rex replied. "See if you can do anything with these ropes around my hands."

"Best let me do it,"Neville interjected. "These are sailing knots."

Rex and Clark were happy to put themselves in his knowledgeable hands. The men watched closely while he manoeuvred the ends of the rope, threading them back through the knots, until both men were free. With careful coaching, Rex was able to repeat the efforts and untie Neville's hands, as well.

Having full freedom of movement worked wonders on the men's outlook. Yes, they'd been dumped in the warehouse, but at least they were together. Other than a mild headache, they were thus far injury free. Staying that way was their next challenge.

"Have you found an exit?" Clark asked Rex.

"I was hardly going to wander off and leave the two of you lying here insensible. Besides, have you noticed how precarious these stacks of materials are? What is all this stuff?"

Neville stood up and stretched, taking care not to knock into anything. He approached the nearest stack of crates and read the faded label on the sides. Rex squashed the urge to join him, not wanting to block what little light they had.

No longer looking like a hapless puppy, Neville moved around, his practiced eye making sense of the mishmash of materials. He tugged on a drape of material and rubbed it between his fingers. Next, he shoved open a half-closed crate and peered inside. "Hmmm."

Clark elbowed Rex in the ribs. "Is he putting on this show for us, or are you still hopeful he'll get us out of this mess?"

Before Rex could reply, Neville looked up at the ceiling and then quickly scooted around a pile of rubbish to disappear from view. Rex's nerves grew taut as he listened to Neville's tread speed up and then slow down in turn. He was ready to set off in search of the man when he heard him give a cheer.

Neville's footsteps grew louder as he returned to the other men. "I know where we are!" he announced. "This is the old army warehouse on the Isle of the Dogs. I used to play in here when I was a lad. Took me a while to figure out because the last time I was here, the place was only half-full."

"Do you know how to get us out of here?"

"Who would have stashed us here?"

Clark's and Rex's questions overlapped, leaving Neville in a quandary over which to answer first. Clark glared at Rex, cowing him into keeping quiet.

"First we get free, then we can discuss how we got here to

your heart's content, Rex old boy." Clark turned his gaze on Neville, desperation writ large in his wrinkled brow. "Where is the exit?"

Neville gazed again at the ceiling, taking stock of the angle of the light. It was easier said than done, given the dirty skylights. Finally, he pointed off to his right. "I'm fairly certain there's a giant roller doorway over there, with a smaller entry point beside it. Somehow I doubt we'll find it unbarred. Fortunately for us all, I know of a lesser-known point of egress. It will be a tight squeeze, but I'm game if you are."

"Lead on, man," Rex urged. The longer they stood around in the place, the greater the chance their captors would return. He did not want to bet their continued good health on anyone's generosity. Still, he couldn't resist asking some questions while they made their way around the crowded warehouse. "What's in these crates?"

"I checked the labels, and they all seem to be related to the military. I saw crates of clothing, battle gear, spare parts, and even a recovered sailing mast," Neville added, pointing at a thick wooden beam. "Most of it is left over from the Boer War, but I'm sure if we dug around enough, we'd find remnants of our battles. The unofficial military motto is *waste not, want not.* As a result, these items sit in storage, waiting for their turn at the front."

"Let's hope by the time they're needed again, we're enjoying our dotage." Clark rapped gently on the side of a wooden barrel. When Rex cast him a confused glance, he explained, "For luck."

Rex nodded. "Knock on another one. We can use all the luck we can get. Neville, what can you tell us about the surroundings? How easy will it be for us to escape?"

"Contrary to popular belief, I don't spend my time at the docks. Let's take a gander outside and then come up with a game plan. See that masthead? Our exit point is right behind it."

It took some careful shifting around of the voluptuous carved mermaid figurine, but finally the men got to the brick wall. Starting from the ground to about knee height, only a yard wide, was a hinged wooden panel, secured with a thick iron bar.

"This was once an access panel for a coal store, as best I can tell," Neville explained. "The bar should come free easily enough, and then we've got a clear way outside." He stood back and eyed his companions. "We'll fit, barely."

It took a few minutes of further rearranging to clear enough space for the men to kneel and peek out from underneath the access point. Across the way was another brick building whose doors were sealed shut. No help from that quarter. Clark and Neville kept hold of the door and motioned for Rex to risk looking around.

At first, all Rex could see was the broad side of a lorry as it trundled along the paved road between the storehouses. The driver parked a little further ahead and gave a gruff shout. A cluster of men came pouring out of the next building over. They hurried to the lorry and got to work unloading the crates.

With everyone's attention was on the contents of the lorry, Rex dared to take a longer look. There were enough men milling around that he thought it easy enough to pass unnoticed, so long as no one examined them closely. Unfortunately, two of the men were far too familiar for Rex's liking — Arnie and Gord.

He scooted back inside and motioned for Clark and Neville to close the door flap.

"Bad news, gents. I spotted our captors working in the warehouse across the way. Our window of opportunity for escape might be even slimmer than we think. Problem is, we've got to walk past them to get away. Dressed as we are in black tie, we'll stick out like penguins marching atop an iceberg."

Clark cursed under his breath. Rex sat down on the floor and leaned his head against a wooden box. That they needed to get out of here wasn't in doubt. Problem was, if Arnie and Gord spotted them, Rex and his friends would end up keeping Freddie company six feet under.

That sobering thought spurred him to action. They needed a disguise. But where were they going to find a change of clothes?

The answer was staring him right in the face, in the shape of a crate labelled *Coats and Trousers*.

Chapter 22
Dora takes to the streets

Dora shuffled into the kitchen of her Belgravia home and slouched into a chair at the table. She didn't bother wishing either Inga or Harris a good morning, although they were sitting at the table. Nor did she worry about the cook or the newly hired housemaid, both busy with their morning preparations.

In any other noble house, the appearance of the lady of the manor in the servants' quarters would be cause for alarm. Here, it happened with such regularity that it had become commonplace. The explanation was simple. Dora depended on the unwavering support and silence of all those working in her domain. She'd figured out early on that the best way to achieve this was to pay them handsomely and to treat them all as family.

Harris, Inga, the cook, and the maid watched as Dora reached across the table, dragging the sleeve of her Chinese silk pyjamas through a dusting of bread crumbs, and helped herself to the teal ceramic coffee pot. After she poured and doctored a cup with milk and sugar, she reached a slim hand up to massage her temples, hiding her normally placid features from view.

The cook and kitchen maid moved their work to the other

end of the room, leaving Dora to brood in peace. Inga and Harris exchanged worried glances at the sight of their mistress brought low. Harris wiggled his eyebrows at his partner, encouraging her to speak up.

"Are you getting sick again?" Inga asked. "I can fetch a headache powder for you from the pantry."

Dora stopped massaging her head long enough to glance up. "It isn't medicine I need, but a clue. We've been at this for three days now and are barely any further along than when we started. If it were anyone but us, I'd understand, but we're professionals. By now, I'd expect us to have at least a framework with which to examine the information. Instead, we're beating our head against a wall. It's no wonder my head and neck are sore."

"You raise a fair point, but you have to admit we've been hampered by the necessity of keeping half of what we know from Lord Rex." Inga twisted in her chair and plucked a notepad and pen from the nearby countertop. She flipped past the shopping list and smoothed a blank page. "No time like the present to rectify the situation. We've got paper, pen, and time. His lordship won't expect us for hours. Let's make good use of the morning."

Dora perked up at her companion's can-do attitude. She gave the cook a grateful smile when she slid a plate of bacon and eggs in front of her. "Since you've already broken your fast, perhaps you could take the lead on recounting what we know."

Inga made a few marks on the paper before she began speaking. "What if we organise the events into a timeline?"

"As good of a means as any," Dora agreed. She rose from her chair to get a better view of the page. "Why are you starting with an X?"

"For the mystery event that incited Freddie to take action.

He must have seen someone or overheard something that sent him off on the path toward his death."

Dora choked as her sip of coffee slid down the wrong way. "Bloody hell," she spluttered, sending everyone's eyebrows raising. "Of course! How could I have missed that part? I've been like Rex's cat chasing a piece of string without ever considering the ball it's attached to."

"Retract your claws for a moment and let another muscle take over... like the one between your ears," Inga suggested. "Picking up where I left off, even if we don't know the starting incident, we do know it has something to do with shipping. After all, look at everyone with whom he spoke—Neville, Keppel, the sailor with the tattoo, and the visit to the dockworkers' pub."

"Working backward, we're looking for something that is coming into or going out of the London ports. Did you bring the butler's journal and Freddie's diary back with you?"

"I did." Inga turned to Harris and asked him to retrieve it from their room.

He made quick work of the task and was back by the time Dora mopped the last bit of egg from her plate. At that point, they left the cook in peace and took themselves upstairs to the dining room.

Dora sat down at the table and held out her hands. "Pass me Freddie's diary. You can take another look at the butler's journal. Your expert eyes will have better luck identifying anything out of the ordinary."

The room became silent, with only the periodic turning of a page to fill the gap. Harris was the first to finish.

"I can't see any change in the household buying pattern. The food and alcohol orders varied little from week to week. There were no changes in the vendors, either." Harris closed the book and shrugged. "I can't say I'm surprised. If it were connected to Freddie's household, wouldn't one of the servants have stepped forward?"

"One would hope, but not everyone is as fortunate as I am. However, Victor was one of ours, despite playing the role of valet. He complained about being stuck with mundane tasks and said his only excitement was when he counselled Freddie against using a new cologne." Dora rested her elbows on the table, causing the wide silk sleeves to pool around her arms. "So we've got a mystery event, Neville, Keppel, sailor, pub..." Her voice trailed off.

"Don't forget Benedict," Harris reminded.

"Ah yes, Lord Cavendish. How does he fit into this?" Dora pulled a loose sheet of paper from the front of Freddie's diary and ran her finger down the jumbled list of letters. "I take it he's listed as B—?"

"Yes, as best as I can tell. Freddie's secret code wasn't particularly inventive. The mysterious B- was mentioned three times, from what I recall."

Dora checked the dates of the entries. The first was more than a year ago, well before she'd begun planning her return. The second was more recent, around the time Victor moved into the valet position. The last one was the meeting at White's. If Freddie and Benedict were close friends, or even business partners, there was no sign of it here. Strange as well that Rex failed to flag any reason for those two men to interact. Dora could write one meeting off as chance, but three?

Benedict may have told her the truth the night before, but he'd come nowhere near telling her all of it. Why would he act that way? If the explanation was innocuous, there was no reason for him to hold his tongue.

What would make Benedict hold his silence—even if it meant a man's death went unsolved? This was a question she could answer. Despite the intervening years since they'd lived in the same home, Dora knew she shared the same moral code as Benedict. Few things in this world counted more than family. Ergo, if Benedict was hiding something, refusing to tell even the police, then it must be something big enough to impact the family's safety or reputation.

The family ties that bound his tongue were the same ones she could tug upon to loosen his lips. If the truth was at risk of coming to light, Benedict would need her help to keep it from blowing up in his face. Somehow, she knew he was the lynchpin for solving this mystery.

"Harris, prepare the Model T. We're going for a drive. Inga, can you help me dress?"

"On one condition," Inga replied. "So long as you tell me where you're going and what you intend to do there."

"Done. Not that you needed to ask. I was already planning to explain my logic while I changed clothes. If there are obvious holes in my thought process, I'd much rather hear about them from you."

Upstairs in her dressing room, Dora selected a simple brown wool coat and skirt, pairing them with an ivory blouse. She pulled them on with a vicious efficiency in her rush to get out the door. While Inga selected shoes, hat, gloves, and a handbag to match, Dora shared her thoughts.

Inga whistled when Dora reached the end. "Confronting your brother for the second time in less than twelve hours is a risky move, but I can't fault your rationale. Since you're heading off in broad daylight, let me get a look at you before you rush out the door." She backed up and surveyed Dora from head to toe and then reached for a chestnut brown wig. "Put this on. Your sun-gold bob is far too noticeable for your choice of outfit."

Dora did as she was told and then hurried down the stairs to meet Harris. He had the Model T out of the shed and was waiting in the driver's seat.

Before she left, she had one last instruction to impart to her companion. "Be a dear and phone the dowager's home, will you? I'm not sure we'll make it back in time for lunch, so best to let them know not to expect us."

Inga gave Dora's wig a last tug to make sure she had firmly fixed it in place and then pronounced her fit. With nothing left to delay her, Dora hopped into the back of the car and they were off.

While it was far too early for the members of the haut ton to be out and about, the rest of London was on its feet. Lorries and buses clogged the road, filling Dora's nose with exhaust while they crept along at a glacier's pace. To keep herself entertained, Dora picked out random faces in the crowd and invented stories about who they were and where they were going. It was a habit she'd picked up during her many travels, needing some way to fill the hours spent on trains, buses, and cars. Ships and planes provided their own unique entertainments.

Dora leaned forward and pointed out first an older man and then a younger woman. Harris played along, either elaborating upon her tales or spinning a yarn of his own. They passed an underground station and slowed again to accommodate the more daring pedestrians determined to dash across the street.

A tall man in a flat cap and trench coat caught Dora's eye.

Harris followed her gaze. "What do you think that man's story might be?"

"Noticed him as well, did you?" Dora's laugh was tinged with evil. "A fine-looking chap at first glance, but a closer inspection will reveal him to be well out of his social class. Wait until he gets clear of the mass of people and then pull up beside him."

Harris arched an eyebrow at her odd request, but he knew better than to question her logic. He spied an open space along the side of the road and swooped into it. When the man in question approached from behind, Dora swung her door open, blocking his path.

"Benedict! What a surprise!" she cooed, before adding in a much darker tone a command for him to get in. When he hesitated overly long, she opened her handbag and produced a pearl-handled gun.

"Best do as she says, mate," Harris encouraged, now wise to the game.

When he still refused to comply, Dora was forced to play her final card. "I'll make a scene."

Benedict's shoulders drooped. He glanced at either side, as though he were hoping for a rescue from the almighty, and then gave up and got into the car.

Dora eyed him like a cat with a bowl of cream, but her expression soured when she got a whiff of him. "My word, Benny, did you sleep in your clothing? I've seen English bulldogs with fewer wrinkles than you. And your cologne!" She waved a hand to push the smell away.

Benedict squared his shoulders and glowered at his younger sibling. He launched into a litany of complaints, starting with her latest disguise and rattling right through to the gun in her handbag.

His words went unheeded. Dora's mind was elsewhere. Specifically, she was sitting in the cafe at Fletchers hearing Victor's comment on Freddie's poor choice of scent.

She breathed deep and confirmed her suspicions. No wonder Benedict was loath to reveal his secret. He couldn't even hint at the truth of the issue without disclosing his involvement in a highly illegal trade.

Dora relaxed in her seat, her headache gone and the day brighter. "Drive us home, Harris. We'll need absolute privacy if we're to convince Benedict to tell us all about Freddie's opium habit."

Chapter 23
Rex makes a discovery

Rex, Clark and Neville had no trouble finding trousers in the right size. It wasn't until the men pulled them on that they discovered why the army had abandoned the shipment. Between the moths and the damp, the seemingly new clothes appeared years old.

"Look on the bright side," Rex said, pasting a smile on his face. "We've got a much better chance of blending in with the dockworkers. I doubt anyone out there is worried about keeping their clothing in pristine condition."

"Certainly not," Neville agreed, laughing at the merest idea. "In fact, we should take advantage of the dust to further enhance our costume." To prove his point, he leaned over and swiped a hand across the top of a nearby barrel, and then wiped it on his cheeks and arms.

Clark shuddered at the sight, but Rex ribbed him until he followed suit. By the time they were done, Rex said even their mothers would have trouble recognising them.

"Forget my mother. I'm terrified of what my valet will say when he gets a look at the state I'm in," Clark moaned. "When he sees I've traded my Italian calf-leather boots for this army issue pair, I wouldn't be surprised in the least if he resigns on the spot."

"If we don't make it safely out of this tight spot, your valet will need new employment regardless of what you've got on. Let me look at us." Rex surveyed his friends, impressed with their quick transformation. Clad only in the old army-issue trousers, boots, and their undershirts, they were a far cry from how they'd looked the night before.

They stashed their evening wear out of sight, leaving no clues of how they'd made their escape. Rex ruffled their hair as a finishing touch and declared them ready to go.

Their plan was simple enough on paper. They would wait until Arnie and Gord were inside the other warehouse. Then they'd crawl out from their temporary accommodation, bringing a few props along to help with their disguise. Neville checked the coast was clear and then headed out first. Rex followed, bringing some rope with him. Clark rolled a small wooden barrel under the hatch to hold it open while he made his escape. When they were all free, they rolled the barrel forward, allowing the hatch to close on its own.

Rex threw the ropes over his shoulder, while Neville and Clark lifted either end of the barrel. Then, cool as ice, they headed off toward the busier end of the building, falling into step behind another pair of men. Neville whistled an old sea shanty while they walked.

Rex felt sweat bead on his forehead, and it wasn't due to the strain of the coil of ropes nor to the temperature. He was nervous, although he was doing his level best not to show it. He scanned the faces of the dockhands as they came into view and didn't breathe freely until he was sure he recognised none of them.

More importantly, not a single man there gave the trio a second look. When Rex and his friends emerged onto the larger thoroughfare, he discovered why. The port was teeming with workers. As long as they were confident in what they were doing, Rex figured they could wander around almost at will.

Their simple plan to run away went out the window. Rex slowed his steps until he was standing beside Neville and muttered a question under his breath. "How far are we from finding someone you recognise?"

"A ways away, and given how we got here, I don't dare approach a stranger. We need to ditch this barrel and get something we can use to defend ourselves," Neville said. "I bet we'll find something in that shed." He motioned toward an open doorway fifty yards away. The door hung wide, the top hinge broken. There was no one else nearby. Rex kept watch while Neville and Clark swapped the barrel for a tyre iron and a pickaxe.

"Keep your eyes sharp, men," Rex instructed. "Although our primary goal is to get away safely, we'd be dense to ignore any clues that might help us assemble this puzzle. More importantly, if you see anyone you recognise, speak up," he added, pointing his last remark at Neville.

The men set off again, keeping a steady pace as they walked along the busy port road. Rex was glad he didn't have to find his way back to where they'd started. As far as he could see, in either direction, stood row after row of brick buildings. To his inexperienced eye, they were virtually identical, identified only by signage and an address number.

He let Neville take the lead, not having a clue which direction to go. Neville aimed them toward the line of smoke stacks blotting the horizon. "The customs offices are that way," Neville explained. "I should see someone familiar there."

It didn't take long for Rex to determine he was out of his depth. He was certain the gulls screeching and swooping above their heads understood more of what was happening on the ground. There was simply far too much chaos for his inexperienced eye to identify what was out of the ordinary.

The mix of nationalities was astounding. Rex heard the singsong tones of the Asian languages coming from a huddle of men wearing long white shirts and plain white trousers. Only a few meters away, a group of Brits were busy divvying a load of cardboard boxes, taking the piss out of one another in a nearly incomprehensible cockney slang.

After wasting a few minutes looking at everything and seeing nothing, Rex decided it was time to try a different tactic. He watched Neville. When Neville's gaze lingered overlong in any one direction, Rex followed the same course. With more focus, he could identify a pattern.

Neville wasn't so much studying the men working on the docks, as the goods they were ferrying around. He'd eye the placard on the side of the building, then the containers going in or out the door.

As they got farther away from their starting point, Neville's attention began to flag. Whatever had caught his eye before, obviously, must have been contained to that area of the docklands.

Clark stiffened a time or two, once even going so far as to avert his face. Rex was desperate to ask him who he'd seen, but it was clear this wasn't the time for questions. Whoever Clark saw, he must not have been confident that they were friendly.

For this reason, Rex couldn't help feeling as though there was a target painted on his back. Despite their change of clothing and the tools in their hands, they wouldn't stand up to close inspection. He struggled to remember Dora's advice on how to walk like a common man, but the memory refused to surface. It was drowned by the cacophony of the bustling port.

In truth, the area was almost a city unto itself. Of course, esteemed families such as Neville's owned a good portion of the buildings and materials. However, the workers' lives were often controlled by gang leaders. Rex desperately prayed that Freddie hadn't got caught up in that kind of mess. Surely, he was too smart to think he could take on a gang lord on his own.

Rex angled close to Neville and spoke half under his breath. "We need to get out of here. How close are we to a rescue point?"

"My family's warehouses are still a ways away. If you think we can trust him, Keppel has an office nearby."

Rex wanted to trust the man, but he wasn't sure whether that was a rational decision or one driven by fear of discovery. It didn't help that he barely knew Keppel other than the few times he'd seen him at some society event.

Finally, he gave up and put the choice in Neville's hands. "Your life is on the line, just as much as ours. Do you trust him?"

To give Neville credit, he didn't rush to a decision either. He took his time, looking around once again at the activities taking place around them. Men buzzed around like bees in a hive, each with their task. Some carried packages and goods, others pushed wagons or drove lorries. Though they varied in height and weight, and even skin tone, they all wore a similar grubby, haggard work. Their lives weren't easy.

Rex felt all the more ridiculous for his attempt to fit into their midst. What did he know of the realities of their lives? Was it any surprise that Freddie got caught out and killed for sticking his nose into their world?

Rex shivered despite the warm sunlight spilling over his shoulders.

"I trust Keppel more than I trust anyone else down here." Neville squared his shoulders and picked up his pace. "We'll need to make the next right. After that, it will be the third building on our left."

Keppel's office was located on a side lane lined with airy

warehouses. Unlike the other areas they'd passed, the men here wore sailing uniforms with their sleeves rolled up to show their sun-darkened skin. Their faces were weathered by the hours spent exposed to the vagaries of mother nature, but they seemed happy enough to enjoy the delights of being on dry land.

The wooden placard swinging above the third building in the lane signalled the offices of Keppel & Sons. Rex watched as the door swung open and a man walked out. It wasn't Keppel — far from it. The man's arms were corded with ropey muscles earned through hours of manual labour. His grey hair was covered with a flat cap, and he carried a portfolio under his arm.

Rex was caught off guard when Neville gave a shout at the fellow.

"Langdon! You're a sight for these sore eyes of mine."

The man spun around and nearly choked on the toothpick he'd been half chewing when he glimpsed Lord Neville, dressed as he was. He chucked the portfolio into the passenger seat of the car and opened his arms in a wide welcome.

When he did so, the sleeves of his coat slid up, revealing a hint of the tattoo on his arm.

If Dora had been there, she'd have whooped in glee at the sight of the vibrant blue waves inked into the man's forearm.

Rex, however, had no idea.

It would be another half hour before he cottoned on to just how important this chance encounter would be to finally solving the mystery of Freddie's death.

Chapter 24
Dora gets the dirt

Dora escorted Benedict through the back door of her home and pushed him into a chair at the kitchen table. "Get some food and coffee into him while I change into something more appropriate for home," she said to Harris.

She bumped into Inga on her way up the servant's staircase.

"Back already? Did you forget something?"

"Not at all," Dora answered. "I stumbled across Benedict mid-route and was able to convince him to come here."

"Really?" Inga reared back in surprise. "He's here? In the house?"

"Digging into a plate of eggs and bacon at our kitchen table. Do me a favour and keep an eye on him while I pop upstairs. I had to twist his arm to get him to come, and I'm not entirely confident he won't slip out once he wakes up a bit."

"Will do. I have to admit, I'm looking forward to making the acquaintance of another member of the Cavendish clan." Inga rubbed her hands together, relishing the opportunity. "Oh, before I forget. I didn't have time to phone the dowager's home."

"It's better that you didn't. Instead of us going there, we

need Rex to come here. Give me a few minutes to get Benedict settled and then you can give them a ring."

Dora took the stairs two at a time, not wanting to waste a moment. In her bedroom, she changed into the nearest item to hand. That ended up being a pair of wide-legged trousers. She topped them off with a capped sleeve blouse, letting her fingers fly on the buttons. Fortunately, she gave herself a last check in the mirror before dashing back out. That was when she noticed she was still wearing the brunette wig.

Finally, spit-polished, primped, and shined, she descended the back stairs and swanned into the kitchen. Benedict was wiping his mouth clean with the napkin, his plate empty of all but a few crumbs.

"I suggest we move to somewhere more private," she said, crooking her finger for him to follow. "Harris, could you bring a fresh pot of coffee to the drawing room when you have a moment?"

"Of course, my lady," he replied with a wink.

Benedict had his back turned and missed seeing Inga roll her eyes at the pair of them.

Dora led Benedict to the drawing room and took a seat on the sofa. Benedict remained standing, choosing instead to explore the contents of the room. Dora kept quiet and allowed him a few minutes' grace before giving a light cough to get his attention.

"You're welcome to visit anytime you like, now that you have my address," Dora said by way of beginning. "At this moment, however, we have a murder to solve. I suggest you make yourself at home and tell me the truth of why Freddie came to see you."

Benedict sat with a recalcitrant frown marring his otherwise handsome features. Dora mimicked his expression, remembering that was an effective way to get his goat when they were children. She crossed her arms and relaxed against the sofa cushion. If needed, she could wait there all day.

Benedict glowered. "How can I trust you? I barely know you."

"Why are you so sure you can't?" Dora quipped back without missing a beat. "Believe me when I say that I am your only friend in this situation. Lord Reginald Bankes-Fernsby will arrive here shortly. He owes you no loyalty and will have little patience for half-truths and lies by omission. Tell me everything and I'll do my best to assist you with covering up the unsavoury bits."

Benedict turned his head to stare out the window, struggling with whether to speak. It was a strange change of place for the siblings. Benedict, older and self-presumed wiser, had often lorded his elder status over his younger brother and sister. Anytime he uncovered proof of their antics, he'd rush to his parents to turn them in. Now he was the one in trouble. Of all the family members he might have faced, his wayward sister was the worst option of all.

Dora studied his body language, watching for any shifts in posture or expression that might hint at his decision. When he clenched his jaw tight enough to make the muscle in his cheek tick, she knew he wasn't going to share. She searched her mind for any leverage she might have. The answer came from a most unexpected quarter.

Inga burst into the drawing room, her eyes wild with worry. "Rex is missing!"

"Missing?" Dora half-rose from her seat.

"Neville and Clark, too. None of them made it home last night. I've been on the phone with their butlers."

Inga's words hung in the air. Dora felt a rare emotion overtake her. Her gut churned and her cheeks flared with utter indignation. The time for games was over.

She turned on her brother and speared him with a blazing glare. "Three more lives on the line! How many good men will you condemn in order to cover your backside?"

Benedict crumpled, his shoulders hunching and his face paling of all colour. He pressed his lips together, looking like a mischievous child being taken to task.

Dora hardened her heart against any twinges of pity. "Tell me everything, right now, or I swear on our grandfather's grave that I will shoot you myself. Inga and Harris won't hesitate to help me hide your body."

Benedict's eyes widened, and he glanced at Inga. She nodded her head to confirm her willingness to lend a hand.

He closed his eyes, huffed, and began speaking in a tone so low that it was barely audible. "We've been home for nearly half a decade. Despite the passing of years, sometimes it's as though we never left the war front. For me, it's the night terrors that are the worst. During the day, I can keep busy, but at night, there's nothing to stop the memories from rushing back. All those years I spent at or near the front lines, watching men die on my left and right. Coming home, being cosseted in wealth and privilege, cannot protect you when the attacker lives in your own mind."

"So you turned to opium," Dora said in a soft tone. "Inga and I, even Harris, we were all there, too. We understand far too well how great the desire to float away can be. I take it Freddie knew of your habit."

"Indeed. We served together at one point. Did Freddie tell you that? I was his commanding officer. He came to me and asked how I lived with it all. His suffering was so great, I couldn't hold back, even if the toll the drug takes is almost greater than the solace it offers in return."

"The toll *is* greater," Inga interjected. "Do not fool yourself, Lord Benedict."

Dora cast a quelling glance at her friend and motioned for

her to stay quiet. "Inga is right, but now isn't the time for judgment. You thought you were doing Freddie a favour. What went wrong?"

"It is more a question of what went right. I gave Freddie the address of a place he could go. I saw him there a time or two, so I am sure he followed my advice. But then something changed in his life, around two months back. He decided he needed to be free of the habit. He told me he'd found another way to serve our homeland, and he needed to break free from morphia's hold in order to do it." Benedict lifted his gaze and studied his sister. "I suppose that had something to do with you?"

"Perhaps," Dora answered, refusing to give anything away. "But right now, our focus is on Freddie. If he gave up the drug, why did he end up dead?"

Benedict gave a dark chuckle. "Ironic, isn't it? Let me tell you, the drug holds you in a tight embrace and it is nearly impossible to quit on your own. Freddie asked around and learned of a Chinese bathhouse that offered help. It was owned by a man who watched his brother die of the addiction. He was one of the few in London with both the knowledge and the fortitude to see someone through the battle for freedom."

Dora fought the urge to reach out a hand to her brother. "I note you speak of this man in the past tense. What happened to him?"

"Some new major player in the opium trade disagreed with his service offering. Freddie was there on the night the ruffians invaded the place. He hid in a cupboard and watched his one hope for salvation die before his eyes." Benedict swallowed and then hung his head. "Freddie knew the risks of intervening, but he was like a dog with a bone. He came to me for help and I counselled him to stay out of it. When it was clear he wasn't going to let it go, I pointed him toward Lords Neville and Keppel. If he intended to wade into the quagmire of crime in the docklands, he could find no better allies."

"Only if he told them the full truth of what he was doing," Dora countered. "Instead, like you, he restricted his words to vagaries and broad questions. Then he hied off on his own and paid for his poor decision with his life. At least now I can see the full story. Let us hope, for all our sake, that Keppel remains untouched. He is now our only hope for finding Rex and the others alive."

Benedict hung his head in shame. Dora left him sitting there, with Inga keeping watch, and went into the hallway to use the phone. She barely had time to lift it from the hall table before she heard a fierce knocking on her door.

She rushed over to it, mentally bracing herself for whatever strange turn life was about to throw her way, and opened it.

Such a glorious sight filled her eyes. Rex, Clark, and even Neville, grubby but hale, stood on her doorstep. Her resulting cry of relief sent Inga and Harris rushing to her aid.

"Let them in, Theodora," Inga hissed. "And hurry!"

Dora jolted into action and waved the men inside. It was then that she noticed they were accompanied by a fourth man, a sailor, if she wasn't mistaken. The unexpected addition sent her reeling even further.

Inga led the men into the drawing room and Dora hurried to keep up. Inside, Dora found Benedict frozen in his chair, looking like a deer in a meadow at the first yelp of the baying hounds. She could see the situation required a firm hand, so she suggested they all take a seat and she proceeded with the introduction.

"Lords Rex, Neville, and Clark, I cannot tell you how relieved I am to see you whole. We'd heard from your households that you didn't make it home last night, and we feared the worst. That's why I rang Lord Benedict and asked him to come here. We were about to set out in search of you."

Benedict's head snapped up when Dora said his name in such a formal manner. What had he expected her to do? She didn't dare so much as hint at their connection to one another.

In any case, no further explanation was required, as Rex and the others took her words at face value.

Dora guided the conversation onto safer ground. "I can tell by the state of you that you've had an adventure. I'm also curious as to the identity of our mystery guest."

"Moses Langdon, at your service, ma'am. I work for Lord Keppel," the sailor said, remembering then to take his cap from his head.

When he lifted his hand and revealed a part of the tattoo on his arm, Dora nearly choked. It couldn't possibly be the same man she'd sent Victor to find? After all, she hadn't shared any word of his existence with Rex. But yet, there he was, sitting in her drawing room, without so much as a by your leave.

Dora crossed the room to give herself a moment to pull together and then sat in the vacant wing chair near the fireplace. Once again in full control of her expressions, she smiled benevolently at her guests and asked Inga to ring for tea.

"With this assembly of the minds, I am sure we can finally get to the bottom of dear Freddie's death. Please, gentlemen, tell us what happened to you."

Chapter 25
The identity revealed

Over tea and breakfast breads, Rex recounted their adventures, starting from the fake automobile accident, through waking up in the old army warehouse, and finally arriving at Lord Keppel's office, where they met Langdon. He ended by saying, "I confess that although I walked the docks with Neville and Clark, I'm sure they understood more than I did. Bumping into Langdon was a strike of good fortune, in more ways than one. You see, Langdon was one of the last people to see Freddie alive."

"Really!" Dora raised her hand to her chest and blinked a few times at the news. "What did Freddie say?"

Langdon cleared his throat, uncomfortable being the centre of attention among such an august group. "He asked me whether I'd overheard any rumours about illegal activities. He was convinced someone was smuggling illicit items into the port, and he wanted to learn how."

Dora took the answer in stride. "Were you able to give him the information he wanted?"

Langdon sucked on his lips and shook his head. "Not in full, but I told him what I could. Some of the dock workers talking about a way to earn easy money. All they had to do was turn up for an hour of work before their normal shifts started. Freddie pestered me for any details. I asked around, pretending to be interested in getting involved, and got the name of a pub where I should go. The blokes said the ringleader was using one of the upstairs rooms as an office. He was there every Friday night. I jotted the info on a note and sent it to Lord Frederick's home. Told him that if he waited a week, I'd accompany him to check it out."

"The pub in question is the Ten Bells," Rex said, unable to hold back.

Dora smiled at his enthusiasm. "I suspected as much."

Langdon waved his hands to get their attention. "Don't any of you be getting it in your head to go. Lord Frederick didn't listen to me, and he ended up dead. You're better off keep your nose clean than wading into the turf wars in the city's underbelly."

"He's right," Neville said. "The more I find out about this situation, the less interest I have in digging further."

Dora stood from her chair and moved to the front of the room. "Sitting back is a luxury some of us in this room don't have. Since the moment Lord Rex knocked on my front door, we've been shot at, chased around London, and the three of you were kidnapped. Even if we don't know who this gang leader is, they clearly are cognisant of our identities."

Langdon and Neville squirmed uncomfortably in their seats, recognising they'd been taken to task.

Rex watched his friends' faces, hoping to see a flicker of an idea from any of them. He hated to admit it, but they were out of their depth. As a last hope, he turned to Dora. He didn't know why he expected her to have an answer, but he asked the question, anyway. "What do you suggest we do?"

She crossed her arms and met his gaze head on. "We sit here

and review all the clues we've gathered. I suspect the killer will end up being someone familiar to us."

Benedict spun in his chair and stared up at Dora in disbelief. "Why on God's green earth would you think that?"

"Simple logic, Lord Benedict. You'll call me silly, I'm sure, but I've done little more than contemplate this question for the last several days. Discovering that you three were kidnapped sealed it for me. Somehow, whoever is behind this, has followed our every move, despite our efforts to cover up our actions. They've been spying on us from the moment Lord Rex turned up on my doorstep three days ago."

Rex turned a terrible shade of puce at this news. He wanted to argue against her logic, but it was the only thing that made sense. How could he have been so blind to the truth?

He bowed his head and offered Dora an apology. "I dragged you into this, and put your life at risk. I'll understand if you can never forgive me."

"Fiddlesticks," Dora said. "You only have to glance at the society pages to see proof of how much I thrive on adventures. I'm here, hale, and honestly grateful you've allowed me to play a minor role in this situation. Freddie promised he'd introduce me to his friends. This isn't what he meant, but it's worked out all the same."

Rex gave Dora a grateful smile, but Benedict interrupted their exchange. "Save the niceties for later. I'm the last to the party, but now that I am here, I have every intention of getting to the bottom of this mystery. Will one of you please explain things to me? When did someone shoot at you?"

"Four days ago," Dora answered. "But that's skipping ahead. If we're going to solve this, we need to go back to the very beginning... and that's with Freddie. Before the rest of you arrived, Lord Benedict was kind enough to tell me why Freddie sought him out. It seems Freddie had an addiction, and he consulted his former commander for guidance on how to overcome it. Lord Benedict sent him to a place he knew and assumed that was the end. Isn't that right, Lord Benedict?"

"Err, yes, that's the gist," he said, fumbling for his words.

Rex asked himself why the normally forthright man seemed oddly uncomfortable, but Dora continued on with her explanation before he got too far with that line of thought.

"However, it seems one of the opium gangs took issue with this treatment centre. They broke in and killed the owner, stating they were laying claim to the territory. Freddie was there, hiding, and witnessed the event. He went back to see Lord Benedict, who wisely advised him to take the matter to the police."

"But Freddie didn't..." Rex said, finishing her sentence. "Or perhaps he did, and they refused to listen. It's no matter either way. Freddie would have felt compelled to seek justice."

Benedict spoke next. "Freddie was determined to unmask the identity of the new gang leader. He asked me who would know more about the import trade. I gave him your name, Lord Neville, as well as that of Lord Keppel, thinking that was the safest course. I presume that is how he eventually ended up speaking with you, Mr Langdon."

Langdon confirmed Benedict's assessment. "And then Freddie sneaked into the pub on his own, determined to gather the last clue."

"I blame myself," Dora muttered. "Freddie and I were due for a night on the town, but I was under the weather. Suddenly, at loose ends, Freddie must have decided to follow your tip. From what I can tell, his plan was to spy and nothing else. Unfortunately, the pub owner caught wind of his presence and alerted the criminals. They shot Freddie when he tried to escape."

"But why did they shoot him?" Rex asked. "It was a rash move that only sufficed to draw attention to the place."

The men in the room shook their head as a one. They were mystified.

"Only one reason comes to my mind." Dora waited until the men all turned her way. "Freddie recognised the gang leader, and vice versa. I've rubbed elbows with plenty of gang lords and mafia bosses during my travels around Europe. If they want someone gone, they certainly don't leave behind a body or a trail of clues. They clean up their messes. I'm almost positive this new leader is not a professional."

"If Freddie recognised the man, we must, too. So who is it?" Neville blurted.

"We'll get there, but only if we work through the clues methodically," Dora replied. "We've been through Freddie's last days. Now, let's compare them to our own. Rex, that means we begin with you. What did you do when you learned of Freddie's death?"

"I paid a visit to the Yard, to ensure their best men were on the matter. Not that my efforts made any difference, mind you. I stirred up quite a stink, but they dropped the case, nonetheless."

"And then you came to see me, on the very day Scotland Yard announced the case would go unsolved. Your tenacity was nearly our undoing, but thankfully, we seem to have more lives than that cat of yours. Off we went on our own investigation, following the same steps Freddie took. The only way someone could possibly know we were getting close was if they were also aware of how Freddie tracked them down. The question is, who was in a position to see both Freddie's investigation and ours?"

Rex propped his chin on his hand and considered the crucial question. His thoughts ran rampant, but refused to settle on an answer. They needed another clue.

"Mayhap I can be of assistance," Neville ventured. "It

struck me as decidedly odd that they stashed us in the old army warehouse. That area of the port is practically a ghost town. Who would remember that it was there and how to get in?"

"You remembered," Rex reminded him, not unkindly.

Neville waved that aside. "I'm a rare breed. And since I could hardly kidnap myself, my bet is on it being an army man. In fact, I'm sure of it now that Lord Benedict told us of Freddie's vice. That warehouse, forgotten by the rest of the city, sits next to the docks for the ships from Asia. If someone was bringing in opium, they couldn't find a better location. Any senior army man would have a ready excuse for being in the area if they got caught."

Rex found no fault in his logic. If anything, his words triggered a niggle in the back of his mind. "Clark, there were a couple of times today that I caught you turning away from someone we passed. Who were they?"

"Ex-soldiers, and not the kind you'd offer to spot for a round at the pub. I wasn't sure they'd remember me, but I wasn't taking any chances."

"Do you remember what unit they served in?"

Clark pondered the question but said no. "I worked in the housing office. Do you have any idea how many faces I saw? The only reason I remembered those men is because they got reassigned to new quarters after the riots in Épernay."

Rex stared at the Anatolian carpet under his feet, tracing the lines of the intricate design. He wished the pattern of their mystery was half as clear. The multicoloured, knotted threads circled round and round, creating a perfect oval in the middle of the rug. His thoughts followed suit, spinning around in his head.

Now that they understood Freddie's timeline of activities, the steps he took made sense. There'd been a logical progress starting from Cavendish, through Neville and Keppel, and back to Cavendish for the missing piece. Solving that puzzle had taken Dora and Rex several days, with much outside help, and the petty theft of a guest book.

How could anyone have deemed Rex or Dora a threat unless they knew the pair were retracing Freddie's steps? Dora had to be right. This was someone they'd encountered in the last few days... someone who was in a position to see without being seen...

Who was this major player of which Langdon spoke?

Rex bolted upright as the answer struck him. He was so overcome he burst into laughter, hardly able to believe they'd missed it.

Neville tilted his head close to Clark and asked, "Has Rex gone mad?"

Rex laughed even harder, finally resorting to scrubbing his face to get back in control of his emotions. "There isn't a new major player, there's a new Major. Major Hobart. He must be our man."

"The older man we saw at White's?" Dora asked.

"He's the one. I should have questioned his presence at the time. He retired after the war, on a military pension and little else. And yet, he can somehow afford a membership at an elite private club? Poor Freddie met with all of you, right under his nose, and had no idea the very man he sought was sitting beside him."

Neville wasn't as convinced. "Surely there are other majors who are members... the link is tenuous."

Clark laid a hand on Neville's shoulder to interrupt him. "Not as tenuous as you may think. Wasn't it odd that Major Hobart was so up in arms over our harmless prank? He even dared to send a demand for the guest book's return to Rex's grandmother."

"The major made a demand of the Dowager Duchess of

Rockingham?" Neville pretended to clean his ear. "Surely you jest."

"I don't, not this time around, old boy." Clark leaned forward so he could look Dora in the eye. "Do you happen to have the guest book here?"

"Yes, I do. My companion, Miss Kay, brought it back with her." Dora excused herself to get the book and was back in a thrice. "Mr Langdon, you said this gang leader held meetings every Friday?"

"That's what the dockhands said."

Dora flipped through the pages, checking the dates for the last six weeks. "We were right when we said that Major Hobart practically lives at White's. The log shows him arriving in the early evening and leaving late at night, on every day except for Friday. On Fridays, he always leaves straight after supper, including last Friday. He may have moved the location of his meetings, but he hasn't changed his pattern."

Clark scratched his chin. "What do we do now? We can hardly rush to the police with this information. With our reputations for madcap capers, they'll assume this is another stunt."

Rex had been debating doing just that, but hearing the words come from Clark's mouth made him see the futility of such a gesture. He was right. "We're no better off than poor Freddie."

Dora disagreed. "You've got one major advantage over Freddie. You're alive and you're all together. I may be new to London, but even I recognise the strength of the titles to which you men lay claim. Alone, you have little chance. But together, now that is a different story."

Rex's heart soared at hearing Dora's pledge of faith in their abilities. Her words stoked a fire in his belly. For Freddie and all the others who'd been hurt along the way, he would stand firm with his friends and make sure their voices were heard.

He didn't want to wait any longer. Without a word, he rose to his feet and motioned for the others to follow. "Come along, men. Tomorrow is Friday. We've got a chance to catch him in the act. I'm confident we can gather enough evidence to ensure Major Hobart spends his retirement in a new home, one provided courtesy of His Majesty, the King."

* * *

Rex hunched lower in his seat and tugged on his cap. Although he was in a borrowed car, parked under the shadow of a tree, the back of his neck itched. Someone was watching him, but for the life of him, he did not know whether they were friend or foe.

Worse yet, he couldn't figure out how anyone would have found him. As far as the world was concerned, he'd headed off for the seaside with Theodora and Clark. They'd done all they could to make Major Hobart think they were giving up the chase. After a change of clothes, they'd left the train at the first stop outside of London and doubled back into town. He'd been certain no one had seen them, but that pesky itch refused to go away.

He didn't have to wait long to find out who it was. A moment later, the passenger door opened and a young man slid into the seat next to him.

No, make that a young woman. His nose caught the barest flicker of her perfume.

"Theodora!" he gasped.

A flash of light from a passing car revealed her sparkling emerald eyes and cheeky grin.

"How did you know where to find me?"

"A little birdie told me," was all she said. "I must say, I find it terribly disappointing that you planned to leave me out of the final stage of this game. And don't bother telling me it was for my own good. After our trip to steal the guest book from White's, I've more than proven I can get myself out of a tight spot."

Rex couldn't argue with that. Of course, that didn't mean he was on board with the idea, so much as that he'd failed completely in his search for a response. He consoled himself with one fact. "If we end up in another car chase, at least this time I'll be the one driving."

"Oh Rex, aren't you a laugh! There's no chance we'll end up in a chase this time."

Rex twisted in his seat to stare at Dora. "Why do you sound so sure?"

"Because my butler will be driving Major Hobart's taxi. He slipped one of the footman a five-pound note. Not only was he able to confirm that the Major doesn't have a car, but he also arranged for the footman to wave to him when the Major's ready to depart."

"Wasn't that risky?"

"You said it yourself, several days ago. Finding reliable staff who will turn a blind eye and hold their tongues is practically impossible. It's even worse at these private clubs. Worse for the members, that is. I'm certainly not complaining. But enough about that." Dora pointed at the front of the club. "That's him coming out now."

Rex shifted until he had a clear view. It was Major Hobart, all right. While the man stood waiting for a taxi to pull up front, Rex had a moment to study him. Even from this distance, Rex could tell by the cut of the man's overcoat that it was custom made and almost certainly beyond the meagre pension of a retired officer.

A black cab stopped, and the Major climbed into the rear

seat. Dora confirmed the driver was her butler. Thus reassured, Rex hung back far enough to prevent Major Hobart from smelling a rat.

"Where are the others?" Dora asked. "I expected Clark to be with you."

"We split up. Moses Langdon suggested he and Clark follow Arnie and Gord on foot, just in case we have the identity of the gang leader wrong. Neville called one of his connections in the Customs Office. As soon as they get word from us, they're going to raid the warehouse where the kidnappers stashed us. If all goes well, we'll have all the evidence we need to sew up this case."

Dora rapped her hand on the wooden gearbox. "For luck. Is it just me, or is Harris slowing down?"

"He's turning into Canary Wharf! All that knocking on wood you and Clark have done seems to have paid off. What do you want to bet Major Hobart is going to the warehouse?"

"If he is, it will be impossible for him to deny any connection with the drug trafficking." Dora rubbed her hands together as a frisson of adrenaline raced up her spine. "Turn off your headlights and slow down. Now that we know where they're going, we don't want to give away the game before it starts."

Rex did as instructed. They crossed over the bridge that led onto the Isle of the Dogs. When the buildings and signage rang familiar, Rex pulled over and parked the car.

"We can walk from here," he said. He exited the car and flipped up the collar of his coat. This close to the Thames, the air had a bite to it. The heavy smell of rotting fish squelched what little appetite Rex had. Nothing about this place made him want to linger, and that was without factoring in how he'd got here the last time.

He turned around to see what was taking Dora so long. She

was bent over, fiddling with her shoe. When she stood up, she had a pistol in her hand.

"What are you doing?" he gasped, raising his hands in the air.

"Put your hands down, you ninny! This is to protect us from any unexpected guests, not for me to put a hole in you."

Rex released the breath he didn't realise he'd been holding. His shoulders dropped from where they'd climbed up to his ears, but his heart still thumped loudly in his chest. He forced one foot in front of the other and counted the steps in his head, doing whatever he could to find a state of wary calm.

"Psst! Rex!"

Rex spun around. Clark stepped out of the dark alleyway he'd just passed, nearly scaring Rex half to death.

It was Clark's turn to gasp when he spotted the gun aiming in his direction. "Who's that with you?"

Dora swaggered up to Clark and tilted her head enough to give him a glimpse of her face. "You have to ask? You know how much I love an adventure."

Rex raised his hands and whispered, "Don't look at me! She invited herself."

Clark covered his moustached mouth with his hands and shook his head. "You've put me at a loss for words. That's probably for the best. We need to hurry if we plan to catch Hobart in the act. He led you here, right?"

"Yes, we never lost sight of him. Are Arnie and Gord in the warehouse as well?"

"Langdon and I didn't have to go far to follow them. They nipped out for packets of fish and chips and returned here. They have a lorry parked around the rear. If I were a betting man, I'd say they are planning to relocate their stock."

Rex raised an eyebrow and smirked at his friend. "*If* you were a betting man? You spend more on the ponies than Arnie and Gord earn in a month... and that's factoring in their second jobs."

Dora giggled, causing Clark to flush a shade of red. Clark motioned for them to follow him to where he'd left Moses Langdon.

The sailor was kneeling behind a set of wooden barrels, keeping watch over the front entrance to the old army storage warehouse. He turned at the sound of their footsteps and then waved for them to join him. If it surprised him to see Dora dressed as a man, he kept it hidden.

"Evening, Lord Rex and Miss Laurent. You just missed seeing Major Hobart go inside the building. Although, I presume this comes as little surprise given Miss Laurent's butler was driving his taxi."

"That was clever of me, wasn't it?" Dora replied. "What of Lord Neville and the Customs agents? Are they in place?"

"They are, indeed. They've got a man hiding inside. For the rest, they've agreed to give you a few minutes' head start before they swarm in. If you get into trouble before then, shout and the cavalry will arrive."

"Forget shouting. I've got something far more effective." Dora lifted her hand high enough that the pistol was visible in the moonlight.

Clark leaned close to Rex and elbowed him. "I wasn't sure at first, but now I believe she knows how to use that thing."

"There's one way to find out," Dora quipped back. To emphasise her point, she held the gun up to the moonlight, aiming at the ground, and spun the barrel. Just as fast, she lowered it again. "That said, let's hope for all of us that we have no reason to test my skills."

Rex was in no rush to head inside the warehouse. However, crouching behind a pair of wooden barrels hardly seemed like a better alternative. His mind drifted back to the war days and all the myriad of nights he spent waiting for the action to start. This time, he was the one in control. Sitting there would not make the next step any easier. He cleared his mind, filled his lungs with air, and then motioned for them to head out.

There was no one guarding the door, and no one to alert Major Hobart to their arrival. They twisted the knob and let themselves in. Voices echoed from deeper inside. Rex didn't need a map to know where he'd find the criminals.

They were sitting in the open area where they'd dumped him, Clark, and Neville. Rex recognised Arnie and Gord, along with a couple of other men from the Ten Bells. Sitting in place of honour, in a wooden chair, was an older man wearing a military coat decorated with medals. It turned Rex's stomach to see Major Hobart dishonouring not only his uniform but also the lives of the men who'd fallen while wearing it.

He was so focused on the military man that he didn't notice Dora had split off until he and Clark stepped into the open area and Dora wasn't with them.

That was because Dora had other plans. She emerged from between a tower of crates, striding out with her pistol raised. She didn't stop until she had the gun pressed to the back of Major Hobart's silvered head.

In one move, she'd put paid to any thoughts Hobart's gang members might have of defending him. One wrong move and she'd put a bullet through his head.

Or, at least, Rex thought she might. For all their sakes, he prayed it wouldn't come to that. But he wasn't leaving here without a full admission from Major Hobart. He wanted the man to swing for Freddie's death and for his role as a drug lord.

Rex planted his feet, put his hands on his hips, and surveyed the group. "Major Hobart, our apologies for being late for our meeting. I know you were hoping to speak with us yesterday, but the timing didn't suit. We're here now and we're not leaving until you admit what you've done."

Major Hobart raised his eyebrows, but he took care not to shift in his seat. "I have no idea what you mean, Lord Reginald. I'm here catching up with some of my old recruits. A boy's night, nothing more."

"I see..." Rex shrugged his shoulders. "Were you doing the same thing the night Freddie Ponsonby spotted you at the Ten Bells? Don't play dumb with me. You're an insult to the uniform."

Major Hobart was so offended by Rex's statement that he forgot his precarious position. He half-rose, but the undeniable sound of the pistol being cocked stopped him in his tracks. "You know nothing, Reginald," He growled. "Everything I do is for the men who served our glorious land. The government brought them back home, but did nothing to aid their suffering from the nightmares and visions. Shell-shocked, everyone says, and then they shake their heads as though there is nothing to do. But not me... not us! We offer these poor men an escape from their memories."

Rex let the explanation roll off his back. That might have been how Major Hobart started, but he'd long since left his original intentions behind. "I might believe you if it weren't for the evidence of you lining your pockets with the spoils. You got greedy and wanted the entire market to yourself. That's why your men killed the Chinese man last month. Freddie was there, he saw them, and he refused to let it go."

At that point, Arnie turned to Gord and heaved a full-fisted punch into the man's chest. "I told you I thought someone else was there, but you didn't listen! It's all your fault we're caught."

"My fault?" Gord blustered, struggling to catch his breath. "I didn't shoot the toff. That was the Major who pulled the trigger and told us to leave 'em there. Blame 'im!"

Major Hobart's face drained of colour when Gord pointed the finger in his direction. His silence was as good as an admission of guilt, especially when no one else came to his defence.

Rex felt the incredible urge to throw himself at the old man and beat him for what he'd done.

Clark wrapped a hand around Rex's bicep and held him in place. "We've accomplished our task. Freddie's death has an explanation, and his reputation will be redeemed. As for the rest, leave it to the Crown to claim their pound of flesh."

As if on cue, uniformed men swarmed out from behind them, with handcuffs at the ready to take the criminals into custody. Lord Neville clapped both Rex and Clark on the back and proclaimed it a job well done.

It took what seemed like forever for Rex to get free of the agents and the police. He was dragging on his feet and worried about what had become of Dora. He hadn't seen her since the agents stepped into view. It was as though she'd disappeared in a cloud of smoke.

The borrowed car was where he'd left it. However, it wasn't alone. Another black car was parked behind it, and a slender form leaned against his driver's side door.

She'd got rid of the hat that had hidden her hair. In the moonlight, all he could see were her ruby lips and golden hair.

Rex came to a stop in front of the gorgeous woman. Was it only four days ago that he learned of her existence? Despite telling himself repeatedly that he had to remain strong, he'd fallen under her spell. The worst part of it was that he wasn't sure he regretted it.

But now, their time together was at an end. He was reluctant to say goodbye, the word feeling all to final.

Dora beat him to the punch. She raised on her toes and kissed him on the cheek.

"To say thanks," she explained when he raised his eyebrows. "And so you won't forget me. Something tells me we'll be seeing each other again soon enough. If you're up to the challenge, that is."

Rex gulped, too overcome to say a word. He restricted himself to a nod of confirmation and watched in silence as she got into her own car and drove away.

As he settled into his car, he prayed she was right. The words of an ancient Persian poet named Rumi sprang into his mind.

"Your task is not to seek for love, but merely to seek and find all the barriers within yourself that you have built against it."

If anyone in this world could break down the barriers between them, it would be Theodora Laurent.

Chapter 26
Dora cleans house

Ome week later...
     Lord Audley sat in his private study and waited
while the downstairs maid poured him a drink. The heavy
velvet curtains were drawn tight, leaving the room half-filled
with shadows. There was a coolness in the air, left over from an
afternoon of rain and fog.

The maid, dressed in a black chambray frock with a white
cuff and apron, her dark hair tucked up beneath a pure-white
cap, passed the crystal glass of deep amber liquid to his lordship.
"Will there be anything else, sir?"

"Add another log to the fire, and that should do for a while."

The maid bobbed a curtsy and rushed to do his bidding. She
selected a thick log from the stack and manoeuvred it into the
hearth, sending up a shower of sparks when it landed with a
thud. Task complete, she hovered in front of the fire, warming
her hands over the flickering flames.

Lord Audley coughed to get her attention. "The maid
would normally exit the room at this point."

The maid in question turned around and peered at him
with her emerald green eyes. "I'll play my role to the hilt once

our guest arrives. Until then, I'd appreciate an update on the case against Major Hobart."

"In that case, you might as well pour yourself a drink and have a seat, Dora. Standing as you are with your back to the fire makes it appear as though you're walking out of an inferno."

Dora propped her hand on her hip and tossed back her head to laugh. "I enjoy the lick of the flames far too much to walk away. That said, a drink wouldn't be remiss after the deluge I suffered on my way here." She retraced her steps and helped herself to a glass, filling it with a finger's worth of French brandy. She waited until she was seated across from her mentor before she sniffed the aromatic bouquet of the expensive drink, letting it chase the scent of smoke from her nose.

"I know you read the papers, so I won't insult your intelligence by telling you that Major Hobart is now cooling his heels in His Majesty's prison. You want to know if the case is airtight?"

"Yes, I do," Dora replied. "In order to remain above suspicion, I spent the last week flitting around London's party scene instead of getting updates on the police investigation. Did Major Hobart provide any explanation?"

"He stuck to the story that he was fulfilling his patriotic duty to look after his men. If it's any consolation, he did genuinely regret Freddie's death. His men chased Freddie out of the Ten Bells and Major Hobart took the shot before he realised he knew the man."

"I had wondered why he left Rex, Clark, and Neville alive. Still, regret is a poor substitute for a man's life. He deserves whatever he gets." Dora tossed back the last of her drink and rose from the sofa. She tucked her glass away behind the decanter, leaving behind no evidence of her presence in the room. "It's nearly ten. I should get into place."

Audley stretched out a hand and caught her arm when she

walked past. "Are you sure about this, Dora? You have no obligation to take on a trainee. You are supposed to be on a sabbatical, remember?"

Dora patted his hand. "This gives me reason to extend my stay in England. You've never questioned my decisions about whom I add to my team before now. I firmly believe the man has proven himself, but in the end, the eventual choice will be his alone."

Audley slid his hand free, but didn't drop his scrutiny. "You like him."

"I understand him," Dora corrected. "That's much more important to me than feelings. He is tenacious, intelligent, and, more importantly, he is willing to step back when the situation demands someone else lead. Don't get me wrong. He will need training. I am certain I have the skills to transform him from aimless society darling into an asset to our country."

The echo of a loud knock on the front door prevented Audley from saying anything else. Dora tugged on her wig and cap, ensuring they were firmly in place, and then relaxed her limbs until she resembled a demure maid waiting to do her master's bidding.

Walters, Lord Audley's butler, rapped on the study door and then announced their visitor's arrival. "Lord Reginald Bankes-Fernsby is here for you, my lord."

"Send him in," Audley said.

Dora scurried closer to the doorway, keeping her gaze fixed on the ground. She took up position behind Walters, standing ready to take Rex's coat and hat. Rex barely glanced at her, so intent was he on greeting his host.

Walters guided Rex into the study and pulled the door shut after ushering him in. He stopped short of closing the door completely, leaving a narrow gap for Dora to eavesdrop on the conversation.

The angle of the door prevented her from having a decent view of the room. She was hardly the type to let that stop her. To the butler's chagrin, she lowered onto her knees and peered in through the empty keyhole.

Audley and Rex shook hands and then Rex took a seat while Audley poured him a drink.

Dora's patience waned while she waited for Audley to get on with the discussion. The marble floor was icy beneath her knees. The chambray fabric of her maid's uniform offered little padding for her knees. She shifted her weight from side to side, giving her knees a moment of respite.

Finally, the men got down to business.

"I'm sure you're wondering why I asked you to pay me a visit," Audley said.

"You mentioned a private matter. I can't imagine how I might be of use, but I'm certainly willing to do what I can."

"A worthy sentiment, but you must hear me out before you give me a definitive answer. Before I tell you what I need, there is something I should disclose. It is regarding Lord Freddie."

Rex's back went ramrod straight.

"I am aware that you played a significant role in the discovery of Freddie's killer. In fact, if I understand correctly, if it weren't for your tenacity, Major Hobart might have got away scot-free."

"Err, well," Rex stuttered. "I'm sure Neville overstated my involvement."

"Lord Neville was not my source."

Dora held back a laugh when Rex cocked his head to the side. She could practically see the gears turning inside his head, not that he had much hope of figuring things out. Not without a little help, anyway.

Audley set his glass aside and leaned forward in his chair. He lowered his voice, but not so much that Dora couldn't hear him. He might not be a professional spy, but he was still excellent at setting a mood.

"You asked Neville to keep your name out of the papers. Why? Did you not want recognition for your efforts?"

Rex shrugged and gathered his thoughts before replying. "If you're asking about ulterior motives, I fear I will disappoint you. My only aim was to see Freddie's murderer caught. Seeing Major Hobart's capture was all the reward I needed."

"Well said. It is an admirable position. Now, I ask for further honesty. How did you feel about being involved?"

"I... I don't understand," Rex stammered. "Terrified? Enthralled? I'm not sure myself."

Dora rolled her eyes at Audley's obtuse way of asking what he really wanted to know. She understood why he was beating around the bush, but part of her wanted him to come right out and ask Rex the question.

Audley reached the same conclusion. He cast a quick glance at the door, checking whether Dora wanted to intervene. Dora froze in place, willing him on.

Audley breathed heavily and exhaled as though he'd made a decision. "I won't insult you by asking you to keep this conversation a secret. I've known you and your family for years, and trust that your experience serving in the army taught you the risk of letting information fall into the wrong hands. So, let me get to the point. What I am asking, in a roundabout way, is whether gathering intelligence and passing it along to someone else is something you'd be interested in doing."

Dora wished she could see Rex's face, but his back was to the door.

"You mean, officially?" Rex asked. "As in going on missions?"

"Not exactly," Audley said. "There is an official government entity for such things, but that isn't who I represent. I oversee a secondary branch, where we have a network of highly unorthodox informants who gather sensitive information and send it directly to the Crown. We have an open position for a new trainee and believe you'd be a good fit for the role."

Dora held her breath and strained to hear.

Rex shifted in his chair. "Freddie was working for you. That's it, right? He said he had found a calling, but I never would have guessed..."

Dora's mouth spread into a grin. Rex was smart enough to put things together. All he'd needed was a clue.

"Yes, Freddie was involved, albeit peripherally. This matter with Major Hobart was not part of his duties. I had no more of a guess than you did at the start of how he'd ended up dead in Spitalfields. I pulled the police force off the case and assigned my best agent to investigate in secret."

"Wait, what?" Rex was reeling again. "But who? I encountered no one else."

Audley intervened before Rex could wander further. "Set the question aside for the moment. I need a response from you before this conversation can go any further. Do you want to work on behalf of our king? It is a dangerous role, of that I won't lie. If you accept, you will undergo extensive training before setting off on your own. Under no condition must you follow the example of your friend Freddie and attempt to investigate matters without my blessing. What say you, Lord Rex?"

Dora watched as a wave of calm crashed over Rex. His shoulders and posture relaxed as his purpose in life suddenly slotted into place. She knew his answer before he spoke.

"I'll do it, sir."

Audley sat back in his chair and smiled in delight. Then he picked up a fist-sized ceramic bell from the side table and gave it a ring.

That was Dora's cue. She stood and gave her limbs a shake,

willing the blood into circulation. She smoothed the front of her apron and pushed open the door.

"You rang, my lord?"

Rex half-turned to look her way, but quickly dismissed her as unimportant.

This was lesson number one.

Audley spoke again. "Could you send in my other guest?"

"Of course," Dora answered. Instead of leaving the room, she walked deeper inside, crossing the distance between the door and the seating area.

That caught Rex's attention. His expression, now visible, morphed from confusion to concern and finally to outright shock. Dora pulled the wig and cap off her head, letting her red-blonde waves tumble to frame her face.

"Hullo, Rex darling," she cooed. "Long time no see."

Chapter 27
Rex takes a new path

Rex had seen men be so stunned that they froze in place. It happened more than a few times on the battlefield. They'd crest over the top of the trenches and get a good look at the line of enemy guns pointed their way, and their limbs would lock.

Rex had always assumed fear was the dominant emotion behind such a reaction. But when Dora settled beside him on Lord Audley's sofa, angling her body so their legs were bare centimetres apart, fear wasn't what he felt.

Instead, it was coming face to face with something you thought impossible. His mind simply could not process the information fast enough. His entire world view flipped on its head and then spun in a circle.

"You?" he gasped. "But you're..."

"A woman. Yes, I can see you've worked that bit out. You're not the first to assume a woman isn't a threat. If anything, that's my secret weapon. You'd be amazed at what kinds of things you can learn while men are whispering sweet nothings in your ear."

Rex sucked in air and fought to keep his eyes from crossing.

He was still floundering amidst the influx of surprises and now this thrilling woman was talking about men whispering in her ear.

Audley recognised his difficulty. "Give the man some space, Dora. You know how hard it is for men to think straight when you snuggle up against them."

Dora trilled a laugh but did as she was told. She scooted over to the opposite end of the sofa. Rex could still smell her perfume, but it was light enough that his thoughts finally coalesced.

He had a million and one questions for the woman. He blurted the first that came to mind. "Dora? Is that your real name?"

"Of a sort," she answered, not giving anything away. "It's what my friends have always called me."

"Are we friends?" Rex waved his hands to stop her from answering. "Sorry, ignore that. What I meant to ask is why me? Err, why you? How did you become a spy?"

"I got my start in the same way as you, darling. I took it upon myself to ferret out information crucial to preventing a miscarriage of justice. Lord Audley offered me the same choice he just offered you."

"I did, indeed," Audley said. "That was four years ago, and I've never had cause to regret my decision."

Rex did the math in his head. Four years ago, Lord Audley was in Le Touquet, France, in the same location as Rex himself. There'd been no major crimes there... except for the one...

Dora must have read his mind. "Yes, I was in Le Touquet. Freddie's death was the second murder investigation we've conducted together. I must say, it is far more fun working with you in the open than having to hide in the shadows. I even met Mews, kitten that he was back then. By the way, are you aware you have a tell? You rubbed your nose when you lied about the cat's origins and again when you told me the takedown plan. We'll have to work on that."

"Yes, yes, you'll have a lot to learn, Rex," Audley agreed. "But I suggest you save the training for tomorrow. It's late, and I don't want Rex to linger here overlong."

Audley stood and waited for Rex to follow. Rex wanted to stay put until something made sense again, but Audley wasn't giving him the chance. Dora rose as well and went to retrieve the wig and cap she'd so carelessly tossed aside. With a deft hand, she twisted her hair up and pulled the wig on top. Her emerald eyes glittered in the firelight.

How had Rex overlooked her presence? He'd walked right past her, handed her his coat and hat. His face flushed with mortification over his mistake.

Dora noticed his gaze and hurried over to where he still sat. She offered him her hands and pulled him to his feet. "Don't be embarrassed because I fooled you. I've had years to perfect the art of misdirection and subterfuge."

Rex tightened his grip on her hands, hanging on to her like a lifeline. His inner sense of right compelled him to confess his concern. "What if I can't learn? I'm not like you, Dora. The only world I've ever known is this one — filled with drawing rooms and fancy balls. I don't have your life experience to build upon."

Dora's expression softened. She moved closer to him, bringing their connected hands up until they were nearly nose to nose. She whispered, "I can't tell you who I am just yet, but I can at least reveal this much. I'm as highborn as you, fed from the silver spoon and educated by the best tutors in the world. Everything I've learned, you can too. All you need is time and a willingness to work hard."

Rex smiled at her and squeezed her hands in thanks. He

backed up a step and let their hands fall apart. Adrift on a sea of uncertainty and worry, he put on his best face and pretended all was fine. She believed in him.

He could believe in himself.

Maybe.

Dora and Lord Audley sent him on his way, with a promise to get in touch in the next day or so with more information. Until then, he was to carry on with his ordinary life.

Rex put one foot in front of the other, walking a straight line to his Rolls-Royce Silver Ghost. It was the same car he'd driven to Dora's house on that fateful morning, now once again good as new. Rex climbed into the driver's seat and stared, unseeing, out the windshield.

He should turn around and march inside, and tell them both they'd made a great mistake. No matter what they thought, he couldn't possibly be capable of doing what they asked.

Of becoming a spy.

But his desperate desire to try far outweighed his good sense. He wanted to do something meaningful with his life. God help him, he also wanted more time to spend getting to know Theodora.

No. Dora. That was her name.

He lifted his hands from the wheel and rubbed his face. Only a few minutes had passed and already he was making mistakes.

He forced his hands down and filled his lungs with air. He held it in until the roaring in his ears settled into a peaceful buzz.

He didn't see the cars passing him on the street, nor the few men walking along the pavement. Instead, he pictured himself standing at a split in the road. In one direction sat the chance of a lifetime. In the other, the life he'd known.

His body leaned toward the untrodden path, but whether courage or foolhardiness fuelled him, he couldn't say. Fortune favours the bold, or so they said. His time in the war had proved the truth in those words.

In this case, however, Rex hoped the Roman poet Ovid had it right. He'd postulated that there was more than one goddess who smiled upon those who dared. Fortune, he had in spades. It was the other goddess's attention that he now sought.

He whispered the original Latin line and grasped tight to the dream it inspired.

Audentem Forsque Venusque iuvat — Venus, like Fortune, favours the bold.

* * *

BONUS EPILOGUE -

Did it strike you as odd that Rex's grandmother, the Dowager Duchess of Rockingham, welcomed Dora with open arms? If so, you'll want to read the bonus epilogue to discover why.

With Rex as her new trainee, Dora has the perfect reason to extend her stay in London. But when the Dowager Duchess shows up unannounced, she's forced to think fast on her feet. Can she assure the dowager that Rex's future is in safe hands AND keep her from revealing Dora's secret?

Click here to get the **BONUS EPILOGUE** for free: https://view.flodesk.com/pages/6421acd6d8651e76556a59d6

Want to know how Dora ended up as a spy?

Grab your copy of **Murder at the Front**, a prequel

novella set on the front lines of WWI. As you saw referenced in this story, Freddie's murder wasn't the first case Dora and Rex solved. Murder at the Front takes you back to their start. You'll not only get a twisty tale, you'll also find out exactly how Lady Dorothy Cavendish went from battlefield nurse to Theodora Laurent, international femme fatale.

Get you copy now on Amazon.

Up next: The Missing Agent

The Missing Agent, book two in the Dora & Rex mysteries, is out now. Get your copy now.

Spilled secrets, a dead spy, and a missing spymaster. When your enemies take bold action, there's no room for hesitation.

London, 1922. Theodora Laurent, femme fatale and undercover spy, has spent several months training Lord Rex to be her new partner. It's time for him to undertake his first assignment - finding out who passed along false intelligence to the Cabinet.

Despite Theodora's training, the only thing Lord Rex knows for sure is his spying skills fall far short of hers. However, when London's spymaster himself requests your help, you can't just turn him down.

As a peer of the realm, Lord Rex is the perfect person to take on the search for the loose-lipped politician. Manoeuvring amongst the elite in the halls of Parliament is well within his wheelhouse, promising to be low risk and high reward. Especially, with Theodora at his side.

Or so they think...

But when London's #2 spy ends up dead, their simple

assignment turns into a full-fledged murder investigation with England's leading politicians among the suspects.

Just when they think the situation can't get any worse, someone kidnaps the spymaster.

Can Theodora and Rex uncover the treacherous villain behind the murder and kidnapping before they lose their lives?

Get it now on Amazon.

The Missing Agent
A Dora and Rex 1920s Mystery

Spilled secrets, a dead spy, and a missing spymaster. When your enemies take bold action, there's no room for hesitation.

London, 1922. Theodora Laurent, femme fatale and undercover spy, has spent several months training Lord Rex to be her new partner. It's time for him to undertake his first assignment - finding out who passed along false intelligence to the Cabinet.

Despite Theodora's training, the only thing Lord Rex knows for sure is his spying skills fall far short of hers. However, when London's spymaster himself requests your help, you can't just turn him down.

As a peer of the realm, Lord Rex is the perfect person to take on the search for the loose-lipped politician. Manoeuvring amongst the elite in the halls of Parliament is well within his wheelhouse, promising to be low risk and high reward. Especially, with Theodora at his side.

Or so they think...

But when London's #2 spy ends up dead, their simple assignment turns into a full-fledged murder investigation with England's leading politicians among the suspects.

Just when they think the situation can't get any worse, someone kidnaps the spymaster.

Can Theodora and Rex uncover the treacherous villain behind the murder and kidnapping before they lose their lives?

Get it now on Amazon.

Historical Notes

When I chose to study International Relations as an undergraduate, I never envisioned I'd use my research skills to write historical mysteries. But don't get me wrong - I am not complaining. Falling into the rabbit holes have been some of the most enjoyable moments while writing this book.

I took inspiration for this story from the true tales of the 1920s Bright Young Things. During World War I, society events and the season ground to a halt. Girls who came of age during that time did not get presented to the queen, nor did they have their "coming out". When the war ended, and the living returned home, it was as though all of society was determined to make up for the lost time.

Surviving a brutal, years-long war took an incredible toll on that generation. Having witnessed the horrors of mankind firsthand, their detachment from daily life and resistance to society's rules come as no surprise. Shell shock (now known as PTSD) was a disease to be pitied, but not treated. Men had to find their own ways to survive the memories, and some turned to illegal drugs as a means of escape.

Back then, the only country with any real insights into how

to break an opium addiction was China. It is for this reason that I sent Freddie to Chinatown for help. Everything else related to the deaths and subsequent investigations comes from my imagination.

Historical figures and places mentioned in the book:

Kate Meyrick was indeed a famous nightclub owner in 1920s London. When I read her life story, I knew I had to find a way to include her in my tale. If you'd like to learn more about how a housewife and mother of eight became the Queen of the Nightclubs, Tattler has an interesting article here: https://www.tatler.com/article/queen-of-nightclubs-kate-meyrick-and-the-43-club

Although Dora is my own invention, her international travels include very real references. In the early 1920s, Howard Carter was digging up treasures in Egypt. She very well could have dined in Italy with D H Lawrence and his wife, and almost certainly the upper crust of society would have read his books in secret. As for the further flung trips, the Charles Cottar Dora references founded one of the first big-game safari companies in Africa in 1919. If you'd like to see what Dora experienced, Cottar Safaris is still offering trips today. (https://cottars.com/)

All the exclusive private clubs mentioned in this story are real. White's is one of London's oldest and most exclusive. To this day, it is still only open to men. It took little imagination for me to picture Dora and her friends wreaking havoc in its halls.... and to cheer them on.

Acknowledgments

Writing may appear to be a solitary sport from the outside, but behind the scenes, it takes the support of a lot of people for me to get a book across the finish line.

A huge thanks to the dynamic duo of Ken Morrison and Anne Radcliffe for providing feedback from day one. These two point out plot holes, catch errors, and provide helpful advice anytime I get stuck.

Much appreciation to Brenda Chapman, Joan Newman, Susan Turner, and Fiona Birchall for reading early versions of the book. Their keen eyes were of huge help spotting typos and errors.

The members of my Facebook group lent a hand with naming some of the secondary characters. Thank you, Cyndy Shubert-Jett, for coming up with the name of Rex's valet. Equal thanks to Maria Turner for the name of Dora's butler - with a shout-out to Rebecca Ullah for seconding the motion.

Historical mystery fans might have caught a familiar store name in this book. With Jessica Baker's generous permission, I set a scene in Fletchers Department Store from her Lady Thea cozy historical mysteries. As a fan of her series, it was so much fun to envision my characters crossing paths with hers.

Although Inga Kruse passed away in 2022, her spirit continues to be a guiding force in my life. I hear her voice clear as day anytime I skimp on description. Thanks to her for having stood by my side for so many years. Although Dora's companion Inga Kay is entirely fictitious, she is my way of honouring my fantastically talented and forever opinionated best friend. Miss you, Inga!

I wrote much of this book during daily writing sprints with some of my favourite cozy mystery authors. I want to give a specific shout-out to Catherine Coles, Reagan Davis, Stella Bixby, Eryn Scott, and Julia Koty (aka Natasha Sass) for all their love and support. They collectively fielded all of my pre-launch questions, talked me off a few ledges, and made sure I kept going.

I am forever grateful to my family (mom, sister, husband, and both kids) for putting up with me when my head is in a made-up world.

My heartfelt thanks go out to all of you who read my books. I love interacting with you on Facebook, and receiving your kind emails. Knowing someone enjoys my characters as much as I do is worth its weight in gold.

About the Author

Lynn Morrison lives in Oxford, England along with her husband, two daughters and two cats. Born and raised in Mississippi, her wanderlust attitude has led her to live in California, Italy, France, the UK, and the Netherlands. Despite having rubbed shoulders with presidential candidates and members of parliament, night-clubbed in Geneva and Prague, explored Japanese temples and scrambled through Roman ruins, Lynn's real life adventures can't compete with the stories in her mind.

She is as passionate about reading as she is writing, and can almost always be found with a book in hand. You can find out more about her on her website LynnMorrisonWriter.com.

You can chat with her directly in her Facebook group - Lynn Morrison's Not a Book Club - where she talks about books, life and anything else that crosses her mind.

facebook.com/nomadmomdiary

instagram.com/nomadmomdiary

bookbub.com/authors/lynn-morrison

goodreads.com/nomadmomdiary

amazon.com/Lynn-Morrison/e/BooIKC1LVW

Also by Lynn Morrison

Raven's Joy

Raven's Matriarch

Raven's Storm

Wandering Witch Urban Fantasy

A Queen Only Lives Twice

Printed in Great Britain
by Amazon

37276778R00138